The Reverend Viola Flowers

A Novel

Easter House Press

This one's for you, Ma.

Preface

This novel is one of a trilogy of novels written by the author that examine strong, interesting women at home, at work, at worship, and at play, including their love lives. You will see Rev. Viola Flowers up close as she bravely administers to her little flock in times of joy and sorrow, all while wrestling with the purity of her own faith. The road ahead is often very rocky for her as a woman of the cloth. "God's disciples must have callused feet because of the many jagged rocks they'll have to cross on their travels," her clergyman father told her when she was a little girl contemplating becoming a minister like him. In this story Viola Flowers will find that to be very true.

Chapter One

The hot Southern California sun radiated down on the small house that sat behind some green hedges next door to the church. In the back yard some jaybirds were chasing a crow from the bird feeder. "Vi, are you home?" a female voice called through the front screen door of the parsonage. "C'mon in! I'm here in the kitchen!" Rev. Viola Flowers called to her sister Lettie from the back of the house. Her bright clean kitchen overlooked a back yard full of flowers and fruit trees.

Rev. Viola Flowers, an attractive woman in her early fifties, was the pastor of the Church of God & Spirit, the church next door. Her visitor was Lettie, her younger sister, who had dropped by as she often did after work.

"Why the long face, Sis?" Lettie asked Viola soberly.

"Maxine was here earlier, and we had a big fight," Rev. Flowers said irritably, speaking of her grown daughter. "I don't know what to think of that girl. She's so selfish. She thinks only of herself. It's so aggravating at times."

"What did you two fight about?" Lettie asked, as if she didn't know. "Was it about Calvin?" she then asked needlessly.

Lettie knew Rev. Flowers and Maxine had been quarreling a lot lately over Maxine's repeated rejections of her longtime boyfriend Calvin's marriage proposals. Rev. Flowers felt it was time for Maxine to settle down and start a family, and like everyone else in the family she liked Calvin and believed he would make Maxine a wonderful husband. "He's a nice, responsible, hardworking young man who loves children," was how she described him to friends. But Maxine simply refused to talk about it. On the topic of marrying Calvin she was like a stubborn mule.

"Yes," Rev. Flowers answered Lettie, "She came over here today crying that he's threatening to break off their relationship because she won't marry him. Then she stormed out of here blaming me. The nerve of that girl!"

"You *are* to blame, Vi," Lettie said coldly.

"Me? To blame for what?" Rev. Flowers said with wide eyes. She stopped what she was doing at the kitchen sink, squared her shoulders, and faced her sister with an obdurate look.

Maxine and her Aunt Lettie were very close and shared secrets, going back to when Maxine was a small child, which Viola Flowers saw as natural and healthy for a niece and aunt to be buddies and share secrets. When angry at her mother as a small child, Maxine would pull Lettie by the hand into her bedroom and closed the door, and then she would complain bitterly about her mother. On the other side of the door, Vi would only smile, thinking it was rather cute.

"Calvin wants a family but Maxine can't give him one. That's why she won't marry him," Lettie said bluntly.

"Lettie, what in the world are you talking about?" Viola said in a rising voice, her eyes now not only wider but fearful.

"Maxine *can't* have children."

"What do you mean she *can't* have children? Who says she *can't* have children?" Viola blasted back as though Lettie had lost her mind.

"Maxine's sterile and she blames you."

"Sterile! Who says she's sterile?" Viola gasped, her face hard and her eyes narrowed into tight slits. "What's going on, Lettie?" she demanded to know, folding her arms crossly. She was upset that something very serious had happened to her daughter that she hadn't been told about, and she held her sister Lettie responsible.

Lettie read her big sister's angry face, so she pulled out a chair from the kitchen table and sat down for the difficult discussion to come. Viola took a seat opposite her, clasping her hands before her on the tabletop like an ill-tempered judge at a judicial hearing.

"Do you remember the time when Maxine ran away from home, and I had to go out and find her?" Lettie said.

"You mean that time in high school when she ran away because I grounded her for staying out late, and you found her staying at a friend's house in El Monte?" Viola answered. El Monte was a small town near Los Angeles.

"I lied to you, Vi. Maxine wasn't at a friend's house in El Monte. It had nothing to do with her being grounded. Furthermore, I didn't have to go out and find her. One of her girlfriends called me and told me where she was." Lettie paused nervously, dying for a cigarette but knew her big sister didn't allow smoking in her house.

"Go on," Vi commanded sternly.

"Maxine was pregnant and was afraid to tell you about it," Lettie said, "She knew how strongly you felt about abortions. Somehow she got the name of an old woman in Hollywood who did abortions cheap. She and her girlfriend Pam checked into a nearby hotel, and went and saw this woman. After seeing the woman and the filthy place she worked in, Pam tried to talk Maxine out of it, but Maxine wouldn't listen to her. She was too terrified of you. So Pam called me to come right away and stop Maxine. But I got there too late. Maxine had already gotten the abortion. That poor girl. The old woman had blotched things badly. I got there in the nick of time to check Maxine into a hospital before she bled to death. The doctor at the hospital told her that she would never be able to have children. This so upset Maxine that the doctor had to give her a sedative. The next day she was all right, so the doctor released her."

Glassy-eyed Viola Flowers just sat there stunned by what she had just heard. Her eyes began to fill with tears.

"The real tragedy of it, Vi, was that only one block away from that old lady's house was a free women's health clinic where Maxine could've gotten a clean safe abortion at no cost at all," Lettie said.

"Sweet Jesus! Sweet Jesus! Sweet Jesus!" Rev. Flowers moaned over and over as she sat there at the kitchen table blaming herself, her eyes closed, her head in her hands, rocking back and forth like a spastic person. "My poor baby!" she bewailed over and over.

"Vi? Are you all right?" Lettie asked with alarm at seeing her big sister all broken up like that. Normally Viola was as strong as granite. Now she was like a crumbled graham cracker.

Viola Flowers just sat there, stunned.

****

That night being unable to sleep Rev. Flowers got up in the middle of the night and went into her study and read her Bible. She wanted to find stronger evidence that she had been right in her unyielding stand against abortions. To find stronger evidence that she was only doing God's will. But her biblical search was futile. The Holy Scriptures now didn't seem as unequivocal as in earlier readings.

"Please help me, Lord," she asked God repeatedly as she tried to reconcile the clashing texts in the Bible. In the thousands of hours she had studied the Bible over the years, she had never wrestled harder trying to make sense of God's words. She begged God to help her understand Maxine's predicament without having to think about all the choices that might have produced a different result.

"There was only one choice, right, O Lord?" she pleaded. Then she cried herself to sleep over what she did to poor Maxine and over the grandchildren that she and Albert would now never have.

The year was 2000.

Chapter Two

It was a warm Sunday morning, and although all the windows were open, the church was still hot and stuffy. Rev. Viola Flowers stood only in her slip before the full-length mirror in her office as she was about to put on her ministerial frock to go out to the pulpit. "Not bad for an old gal," she smiled admiringly in the mirror as she stuck her leg out and struck a poise, proud of her still shapely legs and slender ankles. Then with alarm she saw his reflection in the mirror. He was standing in the doorway behind her.

"Oh! Rev. Scott!" she gulped embarrassed, snatching her frock from the chair to cover herself.

The tall handsome black man in the archway turned his head away like a gentleman. "I'm sorry I disturbed you, Rev. Flowers. I was told you were back here in your office and that it was all right for me to come back here."

"Just give me a second, Rev. Scott, and I'll be right with you," she said blushing, holding her frock in front of her.

Rev. Emanuel Scott was an old friend in town to preach at a big revival in the South-Central area of Los Angeles. Known across the country for his powerful preaching, he was the longtime pastor of the New Era Church of God in Christ in Chicago. He and Rev. Flowers were lovers in Bible college, and even today her heart raced a little whenever he was around.

They first met at a small Bible college in Cedar Rapids, Iowa, that they attended just out of high school. They were only seventeen at the time. He was from a small town near Chicago. They were the only African Americans in their class, indeed in the whole school. They both came from a long line of preachers in the black Holiness Movement, a movement that broke off from the Baptist Church in the 1890s for overemphasizing holiness. After leaving the Baptist Church, the leaders in the black Holiness Movement had serious doctrinal differences between themselves and eventually broke into two groups and went their separate ways.

Emanuel's great grandfather stayed with the original group called the Church of God in Christ, the church where Manny's grandfather was also ordained. Viola's grandfather, the Bishop T. J. Crombie, then a young rebellious preacher, went with the other breakaway group that named itself the Church of Christ. Then largely over the issue of speaking in tongues, Bishop Crombie and some followers broke with the Church of Christ and started their own church that they named the Church of God & Spirit. The subdividing of black Christian churches seemed to never stop. When in college Viola Flowers and Manny Scott talked all the time about the possibility that their grandfathers knew each other in the old days, and perhaps worked or fought with each other.

"Good morning, Rev. Flowers," Rev. Scott said, starting anew, "I just stopped by to say hello. I won't keep you. I realized you have to preach in a little while." Being fully dressed now she had told him it was O.K. for him to turn around. "You have a nice crowd out there," he continued, referring to all the people streaming into the church for Sunday service.

"It's good to see you, Rev. Scott. Come in and have a seat. I have a few minutes before the service starts." She pointed to a comfortable armchair, and then took a seat across from him, crossing her legs self-consciously. With his hair becoming more salt than pepper every year, he was handsomer than ever, she thought. "I hear you knocked them dead last night," she complimented him. She had been told that he had preached before a packed house last night, which didn't surprise her since he always drew huge crowds.

He was without question one of the most powerful black preachers in the country. He would have been even more nationally renowned had he been a mainstream minister such as a Methodist or Baptist, rather than a gospel preacher. When about to start his sermon he would get to his feet, walk majestically to the pulpit where he would put his glasses on, and then open his Bible to a silk bookmark. He would read a bit from his selected text, carefully explaining terms and providing historical and geographical background like a college professor.

Then he would take off his glasses and come to rest on his theme for the day. Now the fun would begin. He could preach a whole sermon from just a word or a phrase or two from the Bible that he would repeat over and over, each time adding more context. When he had the right rhythm, he would riff on the theme like a brilliant jazz musician. Then to the excitement of the amen choir, his sermon would increase in intensity and tempo, with the rhythm going round and round like a John Coltrane solo, before folding in on itself and exploding into even more beautiful music-like words and phrases. That would unfailingly bring the worshippers to their feet, shouting hallelujah to God.

His preaching was so powerful and spellbinding that often women fainted. He was a great rapper long before that term was known. His theme always concerned a dreaded sin that could cause the sinner to roast in Hell if not saved by Jesus.

Viola had heard that last night he preached on the Ten Commandant about not coveting thy neighbor's wife. It reminded her of his Nazareth sermon that she liked so much about the farmer and the rich man.

In that sermon, as she recalled it, there was this rich man in a little village not far from Nazareth who lived down the road from a farm family that was so poor they barely raised enough on their smidgeon of land to keep themselves alive. Every day from his doorway the rich man watched the farmer and his young wife trudge by on their way to work in the fields. Despite her tattered clothes and bare feet, the farmer's wife was very beautiful, so beautiful in fact that butterflies would flutter over her like she was a lovely flower.

Late evenings the rich man would emerge from his house and watch the farm couple return wearily from the fields at the end of the day. To the rich man, even though dirtier and dragging from fatigue, the young wife seemed even more beautiful in the evenings. Every day his desire for her grew and grew. He became extremely jealous of her husband and began to hate him for having such a beautiful wife, while he had nobody. He blamed God for this unfairness. Finally his obsession to possess her became so overwhelming that he could stand it no longer. So one evening he followed the couple home carrying a big bag of gold with him.

That sermon and others by Rev. Manny Scott on the evils of covetousness always amused Viola. Rev. Scott had the worst roaming eye of any man she knew. On the eve of Manny's departure for Bible college, when Manny was barely seventeen, Manny's father, a preacher also, warned him with brutal frankness about messing around with the white girls at school. "Son, with you being the only black male on campus, they'll be watching you very closely. Don't do anything that will reflect poorly on the Negro race. So leave those white girls alone." By "they" his father meant the white school officials. Therefore, for the three years that Manny spent at college, he kept his behavior above reproach. For those three years pretty Viola Crombie (now Viola Flowers), a black student like himself, was the only person he allowed himself to have an amorous eye for.

This was remarkable, considering how popular Manny was on campus. By their junior year, despite being black, he was the top man on campus, being voted student president for two years in a row. Males and females alike wanted to be around him—to touch the hem of his garment, so to speak. They were attracted by his fabulous charm. He was particularly popular with the white girls on campus who would flock around him and dwell dreamily on his every word. It was like he was their guru. Some girls came close to swooning when around him, while others brazenly flirted with him. "If he would ask me for a date, I'd just die. He's so gorgeous!" one cute little blonde from Ames, Iowa, told her girlfriends once after Manny had walked by on campus and spoken to them.

When students would gather in groups under the large oak trees in the summertime to study their Bibles, Emanuel Scott couldn't walk across campus without groups of white kids fighting over him to sit down and join their group. And when he did join them, they sat at his feet like dutiful disciples.

All the kids on campus fought over him, save Viola Crombie, the shy pretty black girl always with an armful of books standing alone on the sidelines looking on. Because she didn't chase after him like the white girls did, at first Manny thought she didn't like him for some reason. During their first months on campus, whenever he saw her he would break free from the white kids surrounding him and run to her, but she always rejected him. And he couldn't figure out why. One day he asked her why she didn't like him, and had he done something to offend her.

"You mean why I'm not swooning over you like the white girls do? Well, you don't impress me. You're too conceited and stuck on yourself," she said brusquely.

"No, I mean liking each other like all good Christians should. I'm sorry you find me so repulsive," he said, walking away hurt.

"Emanuel, wait!" she called after him, ashamed of herself for being so cruel. "Since we're the only blacks on campus, maybe we should be friends. But only platonic friends. Nothing more," she warned him.

They became friends, indeed very good friends. They became very protective of each other, often studying together. His popularity with whites on campus, particularly with the white girls, sometimes worried her. "Don't you worry about the Ku Klux Klan?" she asked him once after a white female classmate of theirs, Susie Meyers, had invited him home with her for the weekend so he could meet her parents, and he stupidly accepted. The girl had told her parents so much about Emanuel Scott that they wanted to meet this amazing young black man. Viola had no doubt that the trip was platonic, but that wasn't the point. The point was that where Susie lived in Southern Iowa was a hotbed of Klan activity. Viola felt Manny was out of his mind for accepting the invitation. "I'm not afraid of the Klan," was his cocky reply.

It was amazing how fast they became lovers. Brother and sister one moment, and passionate lovers the next. It happened that quickly. It happened one Saturday afternoon in the college library where she worked and was left alone in charge. Everyone else had gone to the big football game that afternoon. Other than her and Emanuel, the library was empty. She and Emanuel couldn't go to the game because they had choir rehearsal after she got off work.

Therefore Emanuel kept her company at the front desk until she closed the library up at four.

While putting some books away back in the stacks, she had to use a stepladder to put a particularly heavy book back up where it belonged. While on her tiptoes with the heavy book precariously above her head, the stepladder began to wobble.

"Manny, help me!" she shrieked, which brought him running.

He got there just in time to take her in his arms and lift her down. They had been taught all their young lives that you had to keep an eye open for the Devil, lest he would sneak up on you and strike without warning. That was how the Devil worked. While she was in Manny's arms they kissed, a long passionate kiss that seemed to come from nowhere. It's hard to say who kissed whom first. It just happened, for as he held her, their eyes locked, a spark ignited, and, boom, their lips attacked. He let her down and they continued kissing passionately. Having found each other's lips, they wanted more. Her hands explored him, and his hands explored her.

These two young Christian students from a religion where sex before marriage was a cardinal sin, stood there kissing and squirming with desire. Then amid the stacks of religious books and Bibles, they began tearing at each other's clothes as though both had gone mad, with their clothes flying through the air like falling leaves. Indeed they had gone mad, because although there was nobody else there, the library was still opened to the public, with both doors wide open. The Devil had thrown some kind of evil dust in their faces that made them so hot that they had to remove their clothes to get relief. It was an awful situation for two young Christians to be in.

The next thing they knew, they were down on the floor, going at it like animals in heat. After a little pain, the young virgin started moaning softly as Manny pumped deeply inside her. She felt such new and wonderful sensations that she had to fight herself to keep from screaming out ecstatically.

When he rolled off her, still in a daze, she looked around for her panties. She retrieved them but was too weak to put them on.

With her young body still on fire, she wanted only to lie there under the library table for a few more minutes and relish what she was feeling. To enjoy her maiden sex. Suddenly to her utter horror she realized what they had just done.

"Oh Manny! What have we done!" she gasped tearfully. Then to even greater horror, she realized where they were. Bewildered she looked over at Emanuel lying there next to her with his trousers off, struggling to stay awake. How did she get in such a predicament? she wondered. She quickly rolled out from under the table and leaped to her feet. "Oh Sweet Jesus," she groaned as she hastily put her clothes on.

That afternoon they had been very lucky. Except for a girl who unbeknownst to them had dashed in and right back out after leaving some books on the check-in desk, no one else came into the library while they were making love. The girl returning the books didn't know they were back in the stacks.

"Manny, we must never do this nasty thing again. We're only good friends, remember. Nothing more. Do you understand? You must promise," she said to him with tears in her eyes as they walked home that afternoon. She was shuddering, her shoulders shaking, like she had just dragged herself from some cold slimy river.

Feeling the same shame, Manny agreed.

They both promised to get down on their knees when they got home and ask God to forgive them. That night when down on her knees praying, after asking for forgiveness, she promised God that she would be prepared for the Devil if he ever came at her from that direction again. For a few weeks they returned to being only good platonic friends, successfully fighting the physical attraction they had for each other.

Finally, though, the passion was just too strong, and they were sucked back into sin again. They became torrid lovers, making passionate love nearly every day, sometimes twice a day, for the next two and a half years. Despite herself, she fell madly in love with Manny, and he with her. They became engaged to be married, which she hoped would make all the sex they were having less objectionable in the eyes of God.

Then somewhere along the way, at some point after graduating from Bible college, Manny Scott became a terrible womanizer. An attractive woman couldn't pass him without him turning his head and following her with his eyes, and whenever Viola complained to him about it, he would maintain it was innocent. "What harm is there in only looking? You're always telling me I should take more time to smell the roses," he would say, grinning like a Cheshire cat. "She wasn't a rose. She was a little hussy whose dress was not only too tight but too short. And it's not innocent, because where the eyes go, the body isn't far behind," she would reply irritably. Then at some point in their relationship Manny's body started following his eyes, and he cheated on Viola more times than she cared to remember.

Manny's roaming eye worried Viola for another reason. It could get him into serious trouble as a pastor of a church if he didn't change. Going back to her college days, she believed clergymen should keep themselves above reproach at all times. She felt it was morally and professionally wrong for them to take advantage of their position of power to engage in sexual hanky-panky with members of their church. In Bible college she and Manny discussed that problem many times.

"Ministers have a fiduciary duty to their parishioners when administering to their spiritual needs," she argued, feeling that was especially true when ministers were saving souls. "People are so vulnerable when confessing their sins," she said sympathetically.

She was thinking of all the sinners she had observed over the years begging to be let into the Kingdom of the Saved, sometimes sobbing, shaking and moaning like people having fits. Pleading to be lovingly embraced by Jesus, often fainting and dropping to the floor like rag dolls.

"When being saved, people are like small naked children in the bathtub waiting to be picked up, toweled off, and hugged. It's so special. At those moments, sinners are so grateful for finding Jesus that they feel very indebted to the pastor for their new lives. This imposes an awesome responsibility on the pastor," Viola said to Manny Scott once, hoping he would indelibly record what she was saying in his mind. She believed that ministers who exploited worshippers from the pulpit were not only unholy, but unprofessional. In college Manny agreed with her.

"It's preachers like that who give our profession a bad name. It's as unprofessional as a psychiatrist who takes sexual advantage of his mental patients," he said then.

In the early days of his pastorate, when he was keeping his nose clean, Manny admitted to Viola how difficult it was at times for male pastors not to have impure thoughts. "Staying on the straight and narrow can be a challenge," he laughed, meaning the pretty women in the church. He admitted that sometimes when preaching he too found certain young ladies in the congregation sexually unsettling, particularly the pretty teenagers with their short skirts, long bare legs, and flirtatious ways.

Viola knew the problem confronting pastors was much larger than just pretty teenage girls. From the many stories told by her father, she knew that pastors were often the object of attraction from all kinds of women in the church. Spiritually hungry older women with no room in their lives for males, save Jesus and the pastor. Or lonely women with big social holes in their drab lives. Or women so overflowing in their love of God that they sometimes become confused about the physical limits of that love. They see their pastor as a manifestation of God, and would do anything to serve him, including having sex with him. Or just scheming, sex-starved women, often married, who don't mind being physically "serviced" by the pastor every once in a while.

"Every church has such women as members," Viola told Manny. Then she told him to be careful.

It was Manny's philandering that caused Viola to call off their engagement. At the time they were just getting started as ministers. It was a pity too, for they made a great couple. She was so idealistic and optimistic, while he was so charismatic and powerful in his personality. They had planned to work together to make the world a better place. They both opposed war and injustice. Their preaching styles complemented each other's, and their singing voices blended well together. In religious musical numbers their big voices could be heard over the other singers, mixing like a well-rehearsed gospel duet. Most important, their bodies matched perfectly, and just thinking about it still caused shivers to shoot up her spine.

Manny Scott was now the esteemed Rev. Emanuel Scott, noted preacher. Despite their breakup years ago they remained good friends. She looked at him sitting there now, a middle-aged man handsomer than he was thirty years ago. She recalled that shameful afternoon in the library, and those sexual memories made her feel very sinful. Her heart fluttered as she thought of what a fantastic life they could've had together had he not been such a lady's man. "A man with a roaming eye probably has an unreliable heart," her mother told her in their talks about Manny years ago. Her mother was right. His roaming eye destroyed their engagement.

Rev. Flowers glanced at the clock on her cadenza and got to her feet. "I better get out there. Are you staying for the service, Rev. Scott?" she asked him. They agreed years ago that, as a fence to help keep their relationship within proper bounds, they would keep things on a formal basis, hence they referred to each other as "Rev. Flowers" and "Rev. Scott."

"No. I must get back to the revival. I just wanted to come by and say hello. Are you coming to hear me before I leave?"

"Albert and I will try to come and hear you tomorrow night."

"How's he doing?" Rev. Scott asked sourly. Clearly even after all those years he hadn't completely gotten over the fact that this short chunky little business man had taken her away from him.

"You know Albert. He's a Republican now," she laughed lightly.

Without replying, Rev. Scott gave her that look he always gave her whenever her husband's name came up. She read his face. Maybe he was right. Maybe Albert was the penalty she was paying for dumping him. Albert and all his fanciful get-rich-quick schemes. It seemed that every time they built up a little equity in their home, he would come up with a business idea to use it up.

Viola didn't know what was worse, a lady's man or a man pursuing the pot of gold at the end of the rainbow.

"Maybe the three of us can go out for dinner after I finish preaching tomorrow night," Rev. Scott said circumspectly as he turned for the door.

"That would be very nice," she replied tepidly.

When he was gone, she checked herself one more time in the mirror. Then she went out to face her adoring audience. Today she was preaching on sloth.

Chapter Three

That Sunday afternoon as parishioners were leaving the church, Rev. Flowers saw nine-year-old Junior Peterson standing there alone looking like he wanted to talk to her. His grandmother, leaning on her cane, was talking to some other old people on the other side of the church. The boy seemed to be tarrying until Rev. Flowers finished shaking hands with some congregants who were congratulating her on her fine sermon. For the past three Sundays or more she had noticed that Junior Peterson was lagging behind the others after church as if waiting for a chance to catch her alone so he could talk to her. He would approach her timidly, but before she could ask him what was on his mind, he would lose his nerve and run out of the church and join the children playing outside.

Five years ago Junior Peterson's parents were killed in a horrible ten-car pileup on the 405 Highway. His parents were still alive when the paramedics pulled them from the wreckage and put them in an ambulance. At that point that night they had a fair chance of surviving, but they were hauled all over Los Angeles looking for a hospital that would take them, causing them to lose valuable time. "Every night it's the same goddamn thing, Joe. I bet if these folks had insurance that hospital would've found room for them," one of the ambulance medics cursed after they had been turned away from the third hospital that night, all three being the closest hospitals to the scene of the accident. The offending hospitals claimed they neither had the space nor the trauma facilities to treat them. Junior's parents were finally taken to the County Medical Center many miles away, where his mother died that night and his father three days later. Now Junior Peterson lived with his old widowed grandmother who was living on her Social Security.

This Sunday Rev. Flower was determined to discover what the child wanted. "Junior, come here," she called to him before he could turn and flee. The boy looked nervously at his grandmother standing on the church steps, and then walked slowly over to Rev. Flowers.

"Sister Beasley, when you're ready to leave, Junior will be back here with me," Rev. Flowers called to the grandmother who had looked their way. The old lady smiled, nodded in the affirmative, and turned back to her friends. Rev. Flowers took the boy back to her office so the two of them could talk in private.

"Have a seat, Junior." She took a chair across from him. The bright California sun shone in on them through the window. "What's wrong, Junior? Is there something you want to talk to me about?" She waited patiently for him to speak, leaning towards him attentively.

Looking her in the eye for the first time since they went into her office, the boy murmured nervously in a voice barely audible, "Is Grandma gonna die?"

Junior's simple question shocked her at first. She had expected something else. Yet when she thought about it, the question shouldn't have surprised her at all, because many children in their neighborhood, especially the black and Latino children, seemed obsessed with the topic of dying. She recalled the little black girl who came up to her after church a few weeks ago and asked a similar question, except it was about her fourteen-year-old brother. "Is my big brother going to die, Rev. Flowers?" the little girl asked. The little girl's best friend had lost her brother in a drive-by shooting, and the little girl was wondering if her brother would meet the same fate. The little girl's question drew a crowd of children around Rev. Flowers like little chicks at feeding time. It was like they all had that selfsame question in mind about their brothers.

The little girl who had asked about her big brother's dying said something that day that Rev. Flowers would never forget. "Why is God killing all the black children?" the little girl said with great sadness. All the small black and brown faces turned calf-eyed to Rev. Flower in anticipation of her answer, with everyone becoming deathly quiet. The question nearly brought tears to Rev. Flowers' eyes.

"It isn't God, honey. It's the evil men of the world who are killing the little children," she answered apologetically.

"Why doesn't God stop them?" a little fat-faced boy in the crowd asked.

"God'll stop them. I promise that," Rev. Flowers told the children with heartfelt conviction.

Her reply was so silly that it was almost sacrilegious. She regretted immediately what she had just said. "Who am I to be promising what God will or will not do?" she asked herself as the children were walking away," Who do I think I am? I'm a nobody. God's all-powerful and he works in mysterious ways. Only he knows why he does what he does." She felt very ashamed of herself for having forgotten that simple truth. That night Rev. Flowers got down on her knees and begged God's forgiveness for bragging in front of the children. "I didn't mean to offend you, O Lord, but those poor little children needed that assurance," she said sorrowfully, hoping he would understand. Although she didn't say it, she believed that all children in the world needed the assurance that God hadn't abandoned them as it seemed at times.

Now a nine-year-old boy sat before her in her office needing that same assurance. Did she dare give it to him? Should she promise him that his grandmother wouldn't die on him and would be around long enough to help him grow up?

"Junior, I wouldn't worry if I were you. Your grandmother's strong and healthy. In fact she's stronger than many of the men in the church. Remember the time she helped us move those heavy benches?" she chuckled lightly.

"Nanny's strong, all right. She takes the garbage cans out front every Sunday night all by herself," the boy said proudly, his face now one big happy grin.

"Now give me a big hug and go out and play," she said as they both got to their feet. They hugged. Rev. Flowers was pleased that she was able to give Junior some assurance about his future without lying to him.

"Did I tell him right, Jesus?" she asked skyward as the boy disappeared through the door.

Chapter Four

The next night because of Viola's presence in the audience, Rev. Emanuel Scott preached more brilliantly than ever. Preachers, especially the great ones, particularly the fancy Dans like Rev. Scott, are very competitive, and just knowing that another great preacher is in the audience usually brings out the best in them. It's like how great musicians in the audience often bring out better performances from the musicians on stage.

Therefore, seeing Rev. Flower's lovely face in the congregation made Rev. Scott strut and prance in the pulpit like a grand peacock. And his plumage was just as magnificent. His sermon on the evils of temptation had all the brothers and sisters in the church, including Rev. Flowers, shouting hallelujah. Then as was his wont, he ended his sermon by moving seamlessly into song, starting a cappella, then being joined by the pianist, then the choir, and then the whole congregation. The packed South-Central gospel church rocked with wondrous song.

When the service was over, Rev. Scott rushed to her. "I'm glad you could come, Rev. Flowers. Where's your husband? Didn't he come?" he asked with a big satisfied grin. He knew Albert hadn't come with her, because that was the first thing he noticed from the pulpit when she walked in alone. As usual he was amazed by how popular she was. Everyone in church seemed to know and love her. From the pulpit he had watched her squeeze her way politely past folks seated in one of the pews so she could sit with friends in the middle of the aisle.

Watching her daintily smooth her dress under her and open her Bible on her lap brought back fond memories for him of their dating days in college. Erotic memories. Memories of the two of them lying in bed together naked, reading their Bibles while cramming for finals.

He recalled the feel of her soft warm body when it rubbed lightly against his nude body whenever she moved to adjust her pillow or to get more comfortable on top of the comforter. He remembered how it used to drive him crazy with desire when, around break time from their studying, she would start sexually teasing him by rubbing her bare thigh and leg against his bare thigh and leg. It was especially arousing when she did that while pretending to be still reading her Bible.

Viola enjoyed being sexually wicked like that, which excited him all the more. Wearing that devilish smile she always wore when being naughty, she would then take his hand and place it gently on one of her bare breasts. He would turn and begin kissing her, his thing big and hard again. Then they would make passionate love and afterwards go back to hitting the books like nothing had happened.

Rev. Flowers appeared the same now as she did then, except a little grayer and a little heavier. At first her coming to church alone worried him. His dinner invitation had included her husband as well, so he worried that perhaps now, with just the two of them, him and her, she wouldn't go out to dinner with him. He felt much better when he realized that she had dressed for the occasion. She had that extra touch that women always have when going out to a fancy dinner.

"Albert couldn't come. He had to meet with some supporters who want to help finance his campaign," she said awkwardly. She was referring to the fact that her husband Albert was running for Congress, and that his business partner Bob Haines had set up a meeting with some wealthy white Republicans who were interested in backing him.

Bob Haines was her husband's white business partner in the Bright Star Shuttle Company that they acquired a few years ago with a small business minority loan. Their shuttle vans worked mostly out of Los Angeles International Airport, sometimes called LAX.

"I'm sorry Albert couldn't make it," Rev. Scott said, whose words of regret were betrayed by his dancing eyes. "I don't blame him for going where the money is," he joked.

"Are we still going to dinner?" he then asked with bated breath. Mentally he had his fingers crossed. He was delighted when she replied that she was looking forward to it.

He excused himself to greet some of his well-wishers, telling Viola he would be ready to go in a few minutes. While standing there waiting for him, Rev. Flowers chatted with some fans of hers.

****

"Where shall we go to eat?" she asked him as they walked to her car in the parking lot. "I have this member who opened a new restaurant near here that everyone says is very good. He could probably use our business."

Before leaving home Rev. Flowers had decided that she was going to enjoy herself tonight, Albert or no Albert. At home earlier that evening she and Albert had a big argument about synchronizing their respective schedules better, because lately it had become nearly impossible for her to plan anything involving him since he had to clear everything with Bob Haines first. In one of their spates she blurted out angrily, "Who are you married to, Albert? Me or Bob?"

Looking like a puppy dog that had just been scolded for peeing on the carpet, Albert replied hurt, "That's unfair, Vi. You know Bob's my campaign manager. I told you before I accepted the nomination that I wouldn't run if you had the slightest objection."

Viola realized the instant the heated words left her lips that she had been unfair, and she felt very badly about it. Albert had indeed asked her permission before agreeing to run. While she doubted his ability to win as a Republican in their district, she gave her approval. Albert was such an ambitious man. But he was a good man and would do much good if he managed to get to Congress. She liked that about him. Even though he had changed his political affiliation, he still thought like a Democrat on most things.

Even with that said, she had good reason to be angry at him tonight. He had promised to go to church with her tonight to hear Rev. Scott preach on his last night in town. He assented that afterwards the three of them would go out to dinner together. Albert even checked his calendar with Bob Haines to see if he was free for the night. However, at the last minute Bob Haines set that meeting up for him, and of course Viola was very upset about it.

She was angry at Albert mostly because of the predicament it left her in regarding dinner with Rev. Scott later. It wasn't that she didn't trust herself to be alone with Rev. Scott. It was that the situation just didn't need to happen. After thinking about it more, she decided to go alone and enjoy herself. The moonlit night was simply too beautiful to be spoiled by Albert and Bob Haines.

Rev. Scott climbed into the front passenger seat of her car while she went around and got in behind the wheel. "I was thinking of maybe a nice restaurant in the Marina on the waterfront. It's such a gorgeous night out. Maybe afterwards we can take a stroll and look at the yachts. I hate coming to L.A. without going to the beach," he said when finally answering her about where they should go to eat.

She chuckled. She couldn't help it, for he had started to say "a nice cozy" restaurant in the Marina, with "cozy" meaning "romantic." Even after all those years she could still read his mind like a road map. He hadn't changed. She smiled smugly.

"What?" he asked, reading her face. He had the look of a little boy just caught with his hand in the candy jar.

"You know what," the cut of her beautiful eyes said.

She drove off in silence. Why not the Marina? she thought. She had had a rough day. A quiet dinner somewhere overlooking the ocean would indeed be nice. She deserved it. She thought of Albert and Bob Haines and gladly headed west toward the Pacific Ocean.

Dinner was like old times. Manny Scott was his old delightful self. There wasn't a man alive who could be more witty and charming when he wanted to be. More beautiful.

He kept her laughing all night while they were eating, especially his story about Rev. Milton Stiles. Rev. Stiles was a pastor friend of theirs with a church in Springfield, who had the most beautiful tenor voice imaginable. Since age fourteen Rev. Stiles suffered from Tourette Syndrome, a neurological disorder that caused him without warning to suddenly jerk, shout, bark, and curse involuntarily as if controlled by some foul-mouthed demon, a behavior so out of character for this quiet, proper, polite man who didn't otherwise curse or use dirty words. His bizarre tic behavior could happen several times a day, or disappear for weeks or months at a time. It was a urge he had no control over, although he could hold back his tics for hours at a time, which allowed him to live a fairly normal life. But as was typical of people with Tourettes, holding back his tics only led to a stronger outburst later when they finally had to be let out. This often caused him difficulty on long busy Sundays when he preached. And it was always very embarrassing for him afterwards.

Rev. Scott laughed, "For a long time members of Milton's church didn't know he had Tourettes. Then one Sunday while preaching he began swearing like a drunken sailor. The congregation was flabbergasted and many thought he had lost his mind. Then one old sister whispered to the worshippers around her the only explanation that made any sense: their beloved Rev. Stiles was wrestling with the Devil who was trying to steal his soul, and it was the Devil, not the Reverend, doing all that filthy cursing. The old lady leaped to her feet, put up her dukes, and shouted out, 'Kick his ass, Reverend! Kick his ass! We're right behind you if you need us.' Other worshippers likewise jumped to their feet, shook their fists, and shouted encouragement. The Amen choir joined in the sentiment. When it was over, the parishioners said it was the best sermon Rev. Stiles ever preached. Some called it Rev. Stiles' 'butt-kicking' sermon. Now he's regarded as a courageous preacher who'll fight the Devil whenever and wherever he pokes up his evil head."

"Manny, you're lying! That never happened! You should be ashamed of yourself talking like that about someone with a disability," Viola laughed despite herself.

Rev. Scott crossed his heart. "That's a true story, Vi. I swear. If you don't believe me, the next time you see Rev. Stiles, ask him. He tells that story himself."

Manny Scott started laughing again, "A few years ago he told me a humorous story about some parishioners of his who wanted him to officiate at their daughter's wedding. After he agreed to do it, the mother of the future bride asked respectfully, 'You won't bring all that 'fuck you' stuff with you, will you Reverend?' When he told her that he would do his best not to, she replied gratefully, 'Thank you, Reverend. You're a good man.'"

Viola and Manny had another big laugh.

Not be outdone, Rev. Flowers asked him if he'd heard the story about the white minister and his wife who visited a neighboring black church one Sunday and was asked to get up and pray. This was her father's favorite story, passed down to him by his father. It was about the South but she felt it had relevance in the North as well. Because it was a story loose in the black ministerial world, she was surprised that Manny hadn't heard it. She began the story, "When called upon to pray, the white minister got to his feet, closed his eyes reverently, and prayed: 'Oh Lord, my wife and I are so happy to be worshipping here tonight with our Negro brethren and sisters. And Lord, we understand the problems these Negroes face in this life. But they are good Negroes, Lord. So I pray that when my wife and I get to heaven, Lord, our Negro brethren and sisters here will be given seats somewhere in the back of the Kingdom. Would you do that for them, dear Lord? They are fine people.'"

Getting to the punch line, her eyes already laughing, Rev. Flowers said, "When the white minister finished praying and sat down, the black minister got back to his feet and rendered his prayer: 'Lord, you just heard the prayer from our white brethren here, and Lord, you know him all too well. Let him know, Lord, that *if* he gets to heaven, he'll find us Negroes up there sitting where we damned well please.'"

She and Rev. Scott had another good laugh.

Later at dinner, on a more serious note, Viola told Rev. Scott about this young boy in her church who was worried about his elderly grandmother dying on him. "Junior's terrified, Manny. I had a long talk with him yesterday after church to reassure him that there was nothing to fear and that his grandmother would be fine," she said. Tonight she had called Rev. Scott by his nickname "Manny" for the first time in years.

Rev. Flowers continued, "Junior gets up during the night and goes in with a flashlight and checks on his sleeping grandmother to see if she's still breathing. His grandmother says he sometimes lifts her eyelids to see if she's alive. She thinks it's rather funny. When we talked today, she laughed, 'Rev. Flowers, if that boy don't let me get some sleep at night, I will be dead soon.' Sister Peterson really loves that boy."

Rev. Scott commented on how wonderful it was that black folks can find humor in almost anything, even death.

Rev. Flowers suddenly became very serious. "What really worries me, Manny, is that if the grandmother does die, there's nobody left to care for that sweet boy. I've checked. Neither he nor his grandmother has any living relatives that we know of. It's so bad that Sister Peterson has asked me if I would take care of Junior if anything happens to her.

"Are you going to do it?"

"I don't know. I haven't had a chance to talk it over with Albert."

Rev. Scott's handsome face ruffled. "You're too soft, Viola. You've always been. You can't take in every little waif who needs a home," he told her soberly.

There was a harshness in Rev. Scott's tone not really called for by the discussion. The loving, tender way she had mentioned conferring with her husband Albert about the boy had made Manny jealous. That love and tenderness had once been his. Just thinking about it made him sad. This wonderful, intelligent, beautiful woman had once been his, and he foolishly blew it. How does the old saying go about the most wondrous things in life being wasted on the young. Their once-beautiful relationship had been wasted on him. He envied the big-bellied Uncle Tom.

Then Manny felt ashamed of himself for feeling all that animus toward Albert, a man who had never done him any harm. Moreover, Albert was chunky, not big-bellied. Manny forced a smile as a peace offering.

Now Rev. Flowers was upset. "Junior's not a waif! Besides, as Christians it's our duty to be concerned about orphans. Have you forgotten that?" she shot back, now recalling another reason why they broke up years ago. How could a person be so charming and funny, yet so selfish and self-absorbed? Ever since knowing him, she believed that Manny's most serious flaw was his not appreciating that being a minister called for more than just preaching. It required service to others. Most of all, their job called for charity.

Then she smiled and accepted his peace offering. Their dinner had been going wonderfully, so why spoil it now, she reasoned. "You and I, Manny, have always differed on what Jesus expects from us as ministers of God. But let's not argue about that tonight. Where are you preaching next?" she said in a conciliatory tone, changing the subject.

"I'm preaching at the Intergospel Conference next month in St. Louis. Are you going?"

"Indeed I am. I think it's long overdue that we gospel churches start abridging our differences and start thinking about uniting, rather than always splitting up. We're doomed if we don't. Everybody's merging these days. All the different faiths are getting back together again, or are at least talking about it. The Lutherans, the Unitarians, the Methodists. Even the Catholic Church is talking to the Greek Orthodox Church about making amends. Everybody talking about unification except us gospel folks," she laughed.

"Well, it won't be easy. We gospel preachers are so hardheaded," Rev. Scott laughed good-naturedly.

As Rev. Scott was paying their waiter, Rev. Flowers looked across the restaurant. "Manny, aren't those people over there from your revival." The people she was referring to were getting up from their table to leave also. When she and Manny first entered the restaurant, she had noticed this table of well-dressed black people sitting at a window table in the corner, but she didn't pay them any mind since black people regularly dined in the Marina. Manny hadn't noticed them until now.

"That's Rev. Holt and Rev. Armstrong and their families," Rev. Scott said, surprised at first, then breaking into a big grin.

The people across the room spied them and came over. They shook hands gleefully and talked for awhile about what a wonderful revival it had been. Then they praised each other's preaching and compared airline reservations home tomorrow.

"Are you going to the hotel, Rev. Scott? If so, we can give you a lift?" one of the out-of-town ministers said, wanting to spare Rev. Flowers the trouble of driving Rev. Scott back to the same hotel where they were also staying.

Rev. Scott's face fell with disappointment, for he really wanted Rev. Flowers to take him back to his hotel in her car. But Rev. Flowers was greatly relieved; she knew Manny would have found a reason to ask her up to his room had she taken him back to the hotel. And she wasn't sure how she would have handled the situation. Now, thank goodness, she didn't have to make that decision. She was eager to get home to Albert.

Outside in the parking lot as she turned to head for her car, Rev. Scott whispered to her, "My plane doesn't leave until one tomorrow. Call me first thing in the morning. Maybe we can have breakfast together before I leave."

Then they went their separate ways in the parking lot.

"Do I dare call him in the morning?" Viola Flowers asked herself as she headed for her car.

"Oh my beautiful Jesus. Please take my hand," she moaned fearfully.

Chapter Five

When Viola Flowers got up the next morning, her husband Albert was still in bed. He had returned home very late last night from his fundraiser, and would likely sleep late. It wasn't yet six. After making coffee, she piddled around in the kitchen in her housecoat and slippers cleaning up the mess Albert had made when making himself a snack before going to bed last night. Luckily she was able to wipe up the counter before the food crumbs attracted ants.

Sitting there in the kitchen in the quiet of the morning drinking her coffee, she observed through the window a large white globe dominating the sky. It was so white, so huge and so round that it started her at first. In the faint light of dawn it resembled an alien planet that had come down to spy on California. It appeared so close that its craggy surface was clear to the naked eye. It was the moon, full and bright, still hanging around in the unfolding sunlight like it didn't want to go to bed. It was so magnificent that it left her breathless. “More of God’s beautiful handiwork,” she remarked to herself reverently.

She got up from her morning coffee and put her box of recipes back where it belonged. She had taken it down from the cupboard a few days ago to look for Aunt Mildred’s bread pudding recipe that her neighbor Maude wanted to submit to the Pillsbury Bakeoff Contest. The box of recipes had been sitting on the counter since Maude’s initial visit about the bread pudding.

Maude loved cooking contests and entered two and three every year. While she never won any major prizes, she had won many lesser awards, including being a finalist in last year’s C&H Sugar Bake-off in Denver. One entire wall of her kitchen was devoted solely to the plaques, ribbons and awards she had won in various cooking contests around the country.

“This bread pudding’s terrific, Vi. Let me submit it, and if we win anything, we'll split the prize money,” she pressured her black neighbor. Maude had tasted the bread pudding for the first time when Rev. Flowers made it for dinner a while back, and Maude was ecstatic about it. Rev. Flowers thought Maude's idea was foolish, but Maude was so insistent about it that she gave her the recipe.

"With this recipe I'm definitely going to win the Grand Prize this year," Maude said confidently as she went happily out the door with the recipe.

"That's what you say every year," Vi laughed goodheartedly.

Viola felt Maude was excited about her recipe only because as a Northern white person she had probably never tasted old-fashioned bread pudding made like that before. There was nothing special about the recipe. It was just plain old Southern raisin bread pudding that most black women in the South could make. Yet Viola had to admit that her Aunt Mildred's bread pudding was rather special. It was that famous lemon whiskey sauce of hers that made it so scrumptious. She smiled when she remembered what some of the old folks down South said once about Aunt Mildred's breading pudding. When a little girl Viola heard the story from Aunt Mildred herself, who said she was nearly kicked out of her church because of her lemon whiskey sauce. She said that one day her minister sent a delegation to her house to lodge an official complaint about her bread pudding that had become a favorite at the church's bake sales.

"It's not the bread pudding, Sister Crombie. Your bread pudding's fine. It's your sauce. We don't think a good Christian woman like you should be using alcohol in your food. In fact, you shouldn't even have it in your house," one of the deacons said sternly, looking around Aunt Mildred's kitchen like they had been sent to confiscate the booze as well. "All we're asking you to do is change your sauce," one of the sisters in the delegation said meekly, who personally liked Aunt Mildred's bread pudding just as it was, and she always had two or three helpings.

"I ain't changing nothing. If you don't like my bread pudding, then don't eat it. Now you go back and tell the pastor that," Aunt Mildred snorted before showing them the door.

When telling that story Viola would say in closing, "Aunt Mildred said the church took a vote on her bread pudding, and the yeas won handily, which meant her bread pudding could stay in the bake sales."

Rev. Flowers glanced at the clock on the wall. It was still early. She wondered if Rev. Scott was up yet. He had asked her to call him the moment she got up about having breakfast with him before his flight at one. She went out and started watering her flowers. Just thinking about having breakfast with him gave her the jitters. Did she dare go? She knew Manny had a hotel suite, not just a room, because he always insisted on the very best, witnessed by the way he flashed that Platinum credit card around last night. Moreover, she knew he would likely want to have breakfast brought up to his suite. And she saw nothing wrong with that. When on the road she too often had breakfast with friends in her hotel room when she had an early flight out that day. It saved time by not having to dress to go out and it helped with packing.

Dinner with Manny Scott last night had been very enjoyable, she thought. He was so funny. Come to think of it, he had always had a good sense of humor, which was one of the things she liked about him. "Why not have breakfast with him? We're just good friends," she tried to reassure herself as she put the garden hose away. "Besides, I don't have anything scheduled for this morning."

So she went in and called Rev. Scott, then took her shower, dressed, and left a note for Albert that she was having breakfast with Rev. Scott and should be back home around noon.

"Darn!" she said disgustedly when she went outside and found she had a flat tire. She went back in and sat down at the kitchen table with the telephone and called the Automobile Club and was told it would be at least forty minutes before they could have someone there to fix her tire. She pondered whether to call Rev. Scott and cancel breakfast. She felt like crying.

"What's the matter, honey?" Albert said when he saw the hurt look on Viola's face as he stood there in the kitchen doorway in his underwear and bare feet, scratching. He noticed she was all dressed up and looked gorgeous.

“I was going to have breakfast with Rev. Scott. He's leaving this morning. But I have a flat. I left you a note.” She pointed to the piece of paper on the counter.

“Let me slip into something and I'll change that tire for you. No telling how long it’ll take Triple-A to get here.” Albert turned to go back into their bedroom to put on some clothes. Being in the shuttle business, flat tires were everyday occurrences for him.

“Never mind, Albert. There won't be time. I'll call Rev. Scott back and tell him I can't make it. I've already called Triple-A.” Her disappointment was mixed with a great sense of relief. In a way she was pleased about the flat. It lifted a heavy burden from her shoulders. Like last night, fate had spoken again, for there was a part of her—a part she didn't trust—that was just a little too eager to have breakfast with Manny alone in his hotel room. Manny who always had the ability to sexually arouse her just by looking at her.

Instead of having breakfast with Rev. Scott, Viola made a nice breakfast for Albert and herself. As they sat at the breakfast table enjoying a nice chat, she said, “I'm sorry you missed church last night, Albert. Rev. Scott preached a wonderful sermon about the need for us to embrace humility. About how God hates pride because it's the opposite of humility.” She got up and poured them both more coffee. “I hadn't realized there are so many interesting ideas on humility in Psalms, Matthew, and Mark. I think I'll do something on humility next Sunday.”

She put her coffee cup down and said, “After church last night we went to dinner in the Marina.”

“‘Where did you guys go? Fannie‘s Table?” Albert asked, now all ears. Fannie‘s Table was an upscale soul food restaurant in the Marina popular with African American diners, especially out-of-town visitors.

“No. Because the church sisters had fed him so much soul food all week long, Manny wanted something different. So we went to a little French restaurant where we got a window table with a wonderful view of the boats.”

“Is he still married?” Albert asked warily.

He always asked that question whenever Rev. Scott came to town. Albert wasn't a jealous man. His wife Viola was an important religious leader in their community whose job required her to be out among people and travel a lot. He took delight in her adventures. Yet Rev. Scott's many divorces always made him a bit uneasy. With Manny Scott being such a playboy, a husband with any common sense had good reason to worry when he was around. Particularly a husband whose wife's attractive looks still turned men's heads. Particularly a husband whose wife was Manny Scott's first lover.

Albert recalled the difficult time Vi had convincing Manny Scott when they broke up that she no longer loved him and that their relationship was over. Albert didn't interfere because he knew Vi could handle the matter on her own. Nonetheless, it wasn't easy for him to stand by and watch the fire in that torrid relationship wax and wane before finally burning out. Even today he thought he could still smell a little smoke coming from the embers.

Albert looked up at the clock on the wall. "I gotta get dressed, Hon. Bob and I have an important meeting at nine this morning." He got to his feet to leave, then stopped and turned. "By the way, I've some important papers for you to sign." He disappeared into their bedroom to get his briefcase.

"Oh my, what is it now?" Viola sighed with dread as she waited for him to return with the papers.

Since his friendship with Bob Haines, Albert was always bringing her at the last minute documents to sign. Even though she was supposed to be a partner in all his enterprises, she was seldom informed of what he and Bob Haines were doing. Usually Albert was in such a hurry that she didn't even have time to read the documents, let alone study them, simply because Bob needed them right away. That always bugged her. Albert and Bob's dealings were giving her gray hair. A case in point was when Albert and Bob Haines bought their shuttle business. At the time the shuttle business was just the latest of a long line of business ideas that Albert had come home all excited about. But since most of his business schemes never came to fruition, Viola never took them seriously. She had learned long ago that when married to a dreamer, for your own sanity you must take those dreams with a grain of salt, because every month there was always something new, something just as fanciful.

Then one afternoon Albert rushed home excited because the U.S. Small Business Administration had just approved his business loan on the shuttle deal. Earlier he had told her that Bob Haines had special connections at the SBA, but she didn't give that much credence since Bob Haines was such a blowhard. She was rather surprised therefore that they had successfully pulled the deal off. To close the shuttle deal Albert had a briefcase full of papers that he said they both had to sign. "Be sure to sign all the copies, honey," he said, his hands trembling as he handed her the papers.

"Calm down, Albert. Please sit down and tell me what this is all about?" she said about the shuttle business back then.

"You remember the airport van business I told you about. Well, Bob's friend was finally able to get us the loan. I must get these papers back to Bob as soon as possible."

"What's the big hurry? Shouldn't we have a lawyer look them over first?" she replied suspiciously.

"Bob's lawyer has already gone over them, and he says they're O.K. to sign," Albert said impatiently.

"Bob's lawyer? Shouldn't we have our own attorney look at them? Someone who'll look out for our interests, like Bob's lawyer is looking out for his?" she asked irritably. She meant their lawyer Elder James from their church.

Two members of their church were attorneys: Brother Hosea Diggs, a neighborhood lawyer with a small criminal practice, and Elder J.A. James, a well-respected civil attorney with offices downtown. Although Rev. Flowers believed in church members supporting each other's businesses, which the church tried to do by buying goods and services from church members and local stores when possible, she was very reluctant about sending clients to Brother Diggs. To put it bluntly, she thought he was rather lazy and inapt.

"That man's office is so cluttered and junky it's a wonder he's able to find his desk," a dissatisfied client of his, also a church member, told her once. There were stories that he had been sued a few times for allowing important filing deadlines and statutes of limitations to run on his clients' cases. Despite his lousy reputation, for a while Rev. Flowers sent him clients, but had to stop when he badly burned a few of the people she had sent him. It was a pity too, because Brother Diggs was a pious man very devoted to the church and he and his wife seldom missed services. She personally liked the Diggs family. Elder James was just the opposite of Brother Diggs as a lawyer. He had an excellent reputation and his clients were always well satisfied. He was their trusted family attorney before Albert got hooked up with Bob Haines and started using Haines' white lawyer.

"Shouldn't Elder James look these documents over before we sign them?" Rev. Flowers asked Albert again.

"Bob says why pay two lawyers when one will do. You worry too much, Vi. We can trust Bob's attorney," he said with even more impatience.

That occurred a few years ago when Albert and Bob Haines were buying their shuttle business. Now here Albert was again, rushing in at the last minute with a stack of legal papers for her to sign. The only thing he told her about the papers was that they were required for his election run. Her first inclination was to gather the papers up, hop in her car, and rush them over to Elder James so he could look them over carefully, and Albert and Bob Haines would have to wait.

But because Albert looked like his whole world would shatter if she didn't sign that very moment, she reached for the papers to sign them. But as she was about to apply her signature, she stopped with a jolt. She dropped the pen and looked up at Albert with a troubled face. "Albert, is this a mortgage?" she said about one of the documents.

"Yes. We need the money for the campaign," he stammered awkwardly.

She pushed the papers away like there was fecal matter on them. “No! I'm not jeopardizing our home for a political campaign.” She had started to say “for a Republican campaign” but changed it when she realized that she wouldn't mortgage their home again for *any* campaign.

“It'll only be for a short time until some of our larger pledges are fulfilled. We're running out of funds and Bob says this is the quickest way we can raise some cash,” Albert said nervously.

He had hoped she would sign the papers without bothering to read them. He disliked having to ask her to mortgage their house again. It was tough enough the first time when they had to place a mortgage on their home to buy the shuttle business. He knew how fond she was of their small comfortable home. Although it was used as the parsonage, the house belonged to them, not the church. Both pieces of property, while purchased together, had separate titles, with the church having its own mortgage.

“Bob says! Bob says! I don't care what Bob Haines says!” she exclaimed angrily, “This time you've gone too far, Albert! You have no right to ask me to risk our home again! You have no right to gamble with the roof over our heads like in a game of Monopoly!”

“Settle down, Vi. Please. We paid that other mortgage off, didn't we? We'll do the same with this one. We'll pay it off just as soon as we collect the money from all our supporters.” He took out his handkerchief and mopped his brow.

“*We* paid it off? There wasn't any *we*. *I* paid that mortgage off with *my* money. And it wasn't that quick. You and Bob promised me that it would be paid off in six months, and after over two years, you guys still hadn't gotten around to it,” she said to him. She was now sizzling like bacon in a hot skillet. Rev. Flowers seldom got angry, but when she did, she sizzled. She was so upset that her nostrils were flaring.

The business plan for Albert and Bob’s shuttle business provided that the SBA mortgages on their homes would be the first debts paid off once the business got going good, which was why she and Bob's wife Alice finally consented and signed the papers.

When the business got under way, things began to go wrong. First Albert and Bob had been too optimistic about their first year's income and expenses. Furthermore, since neither of them had any budgetary discipline, they kept buying things not in the budget that they really didn't need, so consequently they kept having cash flow problems that caused them to keep delaying paying off the second mortgages on their homes as they had promised. Rev. Flowers finally got sick and tired of all their excuses and paid the Flowers mortgage off herself with some extra money she had saved up from her preaching tours. She felt sorry for Alice Haines who to this day still had to worry about that unpaid-off second mortgage on their home.

"Please Vi. Please. It'll only be temporary. My campaign committee will have plenty of money just as soon as we can pick up all the checks promised us," Albert begged pitifully. He had that look that always melted Viola's heart. It was the look of a sad St. Bernard dog.

Thus as she usually did, she began to waver and feel sorry for him. He was a good man. He loved her and was faithful to her. He was a hard worker, whether at home, at church, or in his businesses. Every day he worked incredibly long hours. In fact he got a plaque when he retired from county government for having never missed a day's work in over twenty-five years on the job.

What she respected most about Albert was that he was not only a dreamer but a person who would act on his dreams. He was a doer, and in her opinion that made him very special, since most people she knew weren't doers. They were just talkers. What's more, he was the personification of the old maxim that: "If at first you don't succeed, try, try again." He had suffered many business failures, yet that didn't stop him. In business he was like a courageous pugilist who keeps getting up whenever he's knocked to the canvass. She admired that unconquerable spirit of his, but loving that kind of person can keep one's blood pressure high.

"Please see me safely through this, Lord. Just one more time," she moaned to herself as she reached for the pen and signed the papers. Smiling that big politician smile of his, Albert stood over her and anxiously watched her painfully apply her John Hancock to the documents.

"Thanks, honey," he said sweetly, planting a big wet kiss on her cheek. He gathered up the papers, stuffed them in his briefcase, and headed for the door.

Bob Haines was waiting for him somewhere across town.

****

The shuttle van business had been Bob Haines' idea. A friend of Bob's had connections that could get their vans into the Los Angeles Airport. At first, still recovering from a failed business venture, Albert wasn't keen on the shuttle van idea. He thought that with all the buses, vans, limousines, and taxicabs already servicing LAX round the clock, the competition would be too stiff. Then Bob Haines told him that the shuttle van company was only step one in his business plan, and that step two was acquiring a McDonald franchise at the airport. That he had another friend who could help them with that as well. "Think about the synergy, Al. The restaurant can feed the shuttle business, and vice versa. It's a natural fit," Bob Haines said.

That really got Albert's attention. He now saw real possibilities of something big coming from it. He had read with admiration about the black guy who owned dozens of McDonald restaurants, and that was the major leagues where Albert wanted to play. Hence he discussed it with Viola at breakfast the next morning.

"I thought you and Bob were working on a shuttle business?" she asked confused.

"We are. There's no reason why we can't own a shuttle service and a McDonald's. Besides, it's going to take us awhile to get a McDonald's franchise," Albert tried to explain.

"Here we go again," a small disgusted voice in Rev. Flower's head said that day, "Why can't Albert stay focused on one thing at a time?" She blamed Bob Haines whom she saw as a wheeler and dealer. But despite that she felt Albert and Bob Haines were putting too many irons in the fire, she gave the deal her blessing.

Thus their shuttle van business was launched with a SBA loan secured by their second mortgages. Now here was Albert asking her to sign another mortgage on their home, this one for his congressional bid. When would it ever stop? she wondered. "Maybe Albert was the penalty she was paying for dumping Manny years ago," she moaned to herself as she got up to do the breakfast dishes.

Chapter Six

Their financial worries in the early days of the shuttle business nearly killed her. From the start Viola opposed Albert's leaving his good Los Angeles County job for a risky business venture like that. She didn't see why that was necessary at that point in the business. She knew many people, including members of her church, who held their jobs while running small businesses on the side.

Take Brother Holmes, for example. During the day he worked full time at the Hughes Aircraft plant, and at night he ran his small machine shop on Venice Boulevard that was growing so fast that he now had four employees.

“I could really leaves Hughes right now, Rev. Flowers, but having a paycheck coming in regularly from my job has helped bail my business out so many times that I hate giving up that job. But I guess soon I'll have to. My business has reached a point where staying at Hughes is now costing me money,” he told her a few months before he quit his job in favor of full time at his machine shop. He said he prayed over it and God told him it was the wise thing to do.

Elder Holmes was just one of the many people Viola knew who had jobs while trying to establish their own businesses.

There were many times when she wished Albert would have kept his government job a little longer. He had owned other businesses while keeping his job with the county, but those businesses were minor and only part-time. With the shuttle business he was forced to retire early from his job because as a condition of their SBA loan, one of the partners had to manage the business on a full-time basis. Since Bob Haines had his hands full with other things at the time, that responsibility fell on Albert. Because the bank loaned them less operating capital than they requested, Albert's paychecks from the shuttle business were spotty at best in the first couple of years in business.

God how they missed those steady government paychecks then, and Albert's retirement checks didn't come close to filling the gap. During that period most of the family's income came from Viola's meager salary as pastor of their church.

Yet it was hard for her to be too critical of Albert. As with bears just being bears when hibernating in the winter, and ducks just being ducks when flying home north in the spring, Albert Flowers was just being Albert Flowers when it came to business. He was a devotee of entrepreneurship. For folks serious about starting their own business, Albert would dive enthusiastically into their plans like they were his own.

Take Maria Sanchez, for instance, a coworker of Albert's at the county. Knowing how strongly Al Flowers felt about people starting their own businesses, Maria talked to him one day in confidence about her salsa sauce.

"Everybody who's tasted my sauce tells me how good it is, and that I should sell it in the supermarkets," she told him at work that day. Albert was her union shop steward at the time. He liked her idea and encouraged her to give it a try. He even helped her with her business plan. She took his advice, got her business going, and it did great.

Eventually to get more space she moved the business out of her small East Los Angeles home and into her garage, and hired her uncle to run the plant as foreman. Then thanks to the Internet, her sales grew so fast that she soon became faced with the inevitable decision of when to quit her relatively secure civil service job to run her business full time. With Albert's encouragement, she took the fateful plunge and quit her job. And Albert was pleased by her success almost as much as she was.

Ambitious folks like Maria Sanchez were Al Flowers' kind of people. People like that at work flocked to him for advice and encouragement. They were like pigeons flocking to a spilled box of popcorn, with Albert being the popcorn. Although Albert loved helping people with their business ideas, he didn't suffer idle dreamers and windbags well. If he felt a coworker was just shooting the bull with him about going into business, he would move away briskly, for he had better ways to employ his time.

In fact it was Albert's passionate entrepreneurial spirit that finally drew him, a Democrat, to the Republican Party. While his old Democratic friends shared his liberal concerns for the disadvantaged and the poor, most of them lacked his enthusiasm for capitalism, which he saw as a great system.

"The Free Enterprise System gives everyone the chance to take a sound idea, save a little money, and open his or her own business, with the sky being the limit," Albert would tell people who would listen to him. He was one of capitalism's most ardent spokesmen. He constantly championed owning one's own business. "If you're going into business when you retire, you need to start planning now," he would tell his coworkers before reciting a litany of things that must be considered, the most important being having adequate capital. "Start saving now," he would advise them.

Albert saw no ideological conflict in his love of business with his support for strong unions. Indeed he believed that strong, honest unions made companies stronger, not weaker. He felt they improved morale, which in turn increased productivity. Even today, on this point he still had heated arguments with his Republican buddies, most of whom hated unions. He also saw no conflict between owning a business and having humanitarian concerns for the working class.

"It absolutely makes no sense in a country as wealthy as ours to have all the poverty and hunger that we have. In fact, it's a drag on the economy," he said when he agreed with his Democratic friends in the old days.

Then he would add a proviso, "I agree with you that government has a role to play in helping the black community, but our community also needs capital so black folks can start their own businesses and redevelop their own neighborhoods. It's true that banks have discriminated against us black folks for years, holding us back, but things have gotten much better now. More of us, especially our young people, should take advantage of those new opportunities and go into business for ourselves."

His old Democratic buddies weren't necessarily hostile to the idea of a black man owning his own business per se. It was only that, to them, this seemed such a feeble way to help the vast majority of black folks with their massive social problems. One friend, questioning the Free Enterprise System's ability to solve social problems, argued, "The Free Market, Al, is driven only by profits, and if something isn't profitable, than the Market wants no part of it. There're no profits in helping the poor, not even for politicians, so everybody runs from that issue."

Furthermore, because most black businesses were barely surviving, many of Albert's old Democratic buddies thought it was the height of folly for anyone to quit a good-paying job to open some shaky little business that would probably never get off the ground. And some of them had unkind things to say about the few black businesses that did become successful, "The first thing a successful black businessman does when he makes a little money is to move out of the black community to a wealthier section of the city, usually a white section, leaving his old neighborhood even weaker," a friend of Albert's said once.

When Albert worked for the county, most of his friends thought he was crazy to leave such a cushy civil service job to enter the risky, dangerous world of private business. Crazy for risking his life savings. They all knew how difficult savings were to come by in the black community. "What's your hurry, Al? Why don't you wait until you retire so you'll at least have your full pension to fall back on if things don't turn out as planned," many of his friends and coworkers would tell him, wanting to keep him from harming himself.

This attitude of Albert's friends and coworkers was very discouraging for him. Even worse, it was very intimidating, because fear held by friends and loved ones can be as contagious as measles. Consequently, due to the timidity around him that even frightened him a little, Albert stayed on his job many years longer than he had planned. At that time had he been around bold, business-minded people like Bob Haines and his friends, he, Albert

Flowers, likely would have left his job much earlier. At least this was what Albert Flowers believed.

"Follow your plan and ignore the worrywarts," he now told aspiring entrepreneurs.

Chapter Seven

Rev. Flowers learned her husband had changed his party affiliation a few months ago when coming home one afternoon she saw strange cars parked in front of her house, with Albert's car in the driveway. She wondered why Albert was home from work so early. When she parked her car and entered the house, she heard him and some strange men out on the patio talking. Even from outdoors the cigarette and cigar smoke from the patio was overpowering. The bottles of liquor, club soda and ginger ale on the kitchen counter made her frown even more, because Albert knew she didn't allow smoking or drinking in their home.

She turned and left the kitchen and went into her office to catch up on her paper work. Albert and the men on the patio were so immersed in politics that they didn't realize she was home. "What's Albert up to now?" she wondered. She was thinking of how Albert and Bob Haines were always working on some big deal or another.

She had just returned from a ministerial meeting across town. Except for Albert and his friends talking loudly outside on the patio, the afternoon was quiet and peaceful. She hoped their loud male voices weren't disturbing their neighbors. Voices carried far at that time of day in their quiet neighborhood. All the men at Albert's meeting were white, and except for Bob Haines, she hadn't seen any of them before.

"This district's been heavily Democratic for as long as I can remember," she heard her husband tell the men on the patio, "I couldn't win in this district as a Republican." The men must have been Republicans. She definitely knew Bob Haines was.

One of the men said, "Times are changing, Al. The party believes a Republican can now win this district. Just look at the demographics. Now the district's almost equally divided between Anglos, Latinos, and African Americans. If you accept the Republican endorsement, we think you can win. The Anglos in the district are mainly conservatives and vote Republican, and as a Republican you would get all those votes. And because of your standing in the black community you should pick up many black voters, despite your being a Republican. Maybe even some Mexican votes."

About an hour later as Viola Flowers worked at her desk in her office, she heard cars departing. Albert's meeting had broken up.

"Guess what, Vi, the guys want me to run for the United States Congress," her husband announced excitedly in the doorway, a big grin on his jolly black face. He was a heavyset, round-faced man with large hands. He had worked for the county government for years before retiring early and going into business with Bob Haines.

"Albert, you can't be serious. You'll never get the Democratic endorsement. State Senator Harris is being termed out and wants that congressional seat. The Democratic endorsement will be his for the asking. He has the unions behind him."

"I won't be running as a Democrat. I'll have the Republican endorsement."

"You're not a Republican. We're Democrats."

"I'm going to change my affiliation," he told her.

"You're going to do what?" Wide-eyed Rev. Flowers put her pen down and got to her feet.

"I'm going to become a Republican," he explained, "I should've done it years ago. I've nothing in common with Democrats anymore. Unlike white liberals, white Republicans don't mind if a black man makes a little money. Republicans believe that being interested in business shows a person's dynamism. A person's ability to get-up-and-go and achieve in life."

He paused and said gravely. "They believe a black man has as much right as anyone to go out and conquer the world. Our white liberal friends don't believe this. They think black people have no business making big money. And they look bug-eyed at black people who do. They believe a black man should always remain with the downtrodden. Remain always the victim. Some even accuse you of selling out just for talking about entrepreneurship. As if being for small businesses hurts poor black folks somehow."

His normally soft round face hardened. "I think you should change your political affiliation also. Republicans are more in line with your thinking on abortions."

"You go ahead and become a Republican if you wish, Albert, but I'm remaining a Democrat," Viola said with disgust in her voice.

She felt that Albert was changing so fast that she scarcely knew him anymore. He hadn't been the same since that day a few years ago when they attended a citywide evangelical conference of mostly white fundamentalist churches. At the conference he met and became bosom buddies with some white born-again men. His new white Christian friends even asked him to join the white Kiwanis Club, where he took up cigar smoking. It was at the Kiwanis Club where he met and became good friends with Bob Haines, a lifelong Republican from Culver City, who later became his business partner. The Kiwanis Club led to Albert's joining other white civic and social organizations.

"I didn't know white people could be so friendly," he told Viola about his new conservative friends when he returned home one day with a bag of golf clubs that one of them had given him. When Vi asked him if he had taken up golfing now, he replied, "Ralph's teaching me. We're teeing off tomorrow morning at the country club at seven," he said with a big smile.

Eventually Albert saw less and less of his old black friends as he spent more time with his new born-again white buddies. It wasn't long before he went into business with one of them. When that business failed, he and another white friend, Bob Haines, established a shuttle service that they managed to get into LAX through certain political connections Bob Haines had at City Hall.

Back then Viola and Albert had many arguments about Albert's new friends.

"Sometimes I don't understand you, Vi. You dislike my new friends even though they're a hundred times friendlier than those haughty white liberals you associate with," he said to her one day.

“I don't dislike your friends, Albert. It's just that—”

Viola Flowers stopped in mid-sentence. It was very hard to explain. In fact she didn't understand it herself. She agreed with him that white born-again Christians did seem more genuine in their friendships with black people than many of their white liberal friends who often came across as phonies. Hypocrites, as Albert called them. White Christians seemed less self-conscious, less patronizing, less fearful of blacks than white progressives were. They seemed more honest in their racial feelings. Maybe it was only black Christians that white Christians embraced this way, she thought. Maybe it was their mutual love of Jesus Christ that made the difference.

Yet in many other ways Albert's new white conservative friends, including their wives, made her feel very uneasy, because too often they seemed to blame poor people for being poor and government for trying to help them, as if helping the poor only deepened their poverty. To her, that was utter nonsense. It was all well and good for Albert's new Republican friends to sat around and boast about how they had lifted themselves up by their own bootstraps, but she knew that for most of them that simply wasn't true. She knew they were always looking for advice or help with how to make money, and if they already had money, then how to make more of it. And there was nothing wrong with that, she thought, for most people needed help to get ahead in life, particularly the poor.

She agreed with the Rev. Jesse Jackson that the less fortunate in life needed a hand up, not a handout. Rich and middleclass people called what they did "networking" or having "connections." But to Viola Flowers that was their privileged way of getting a "hand up," something they wanted to deny the poor and disadvantaged. Albert used to share Jesse Jackson’s views until he started aspiring to become rich.

“Was changing your party registration Bob Haines' idea?” she asked Albert bluntly.

"Bob and I have a chance to get a McDonald's franchise at the airport. Bob thought it would help if I was a Republican too," he answered awkwardly.

Rev. Flowers just stood there and stared at Albert. "What's wrong with those two? Why do they keep hopping from one thing to another?" her bemused face seemed to say, meaning Albert and Bob Haines. Although she didn't know much about the business world, it seemed to her that getting a small business going was much like starting one's own flower garden. First you had to love gardening, which meant loving to work outdoors, loving to work in the dirt, and loving to get plants to grow where you want them to grow. That took knowledge and a plan, for it would be foolish to try to grow things in the wrong place, at the wrong time, and in the wrong way. Most of all, it required learning from one's mistakes. To her, Albert and Bob Haines seemed to be making the same mistakes over and over again. Moreover, they seemed to badly lack the patience needed to get something to grow.

While they always worked hard, they seemed to be always jumping from one thing to another, always trying to add more blocks to a base that was already very shaky. Like with plants, businesses took time to grow, was her opinion. And over the years she had lectured Albert on the virtue of sticking to things until they were done, but he never listened to her.

Now as though their hands weren't full enough, Albert and Bob Haines wanted to own a McDonald's restaurant. They were like many small businessmen Rev. Flowers knew who were never satisfied with the businesses they had. Men who were always scheming to really hit it big with something else. Albert denied that he had a "get-rich-quick" attitude. He would explain in that self-pitying way of his when talking about his business dreams, "You just don't understand, Vi. Just once I would like a business where I didn't have to struggle all the time just to make ends meet. A business that can comfortably support us. A business that can give us those extra little things in life. That's all I want. I don't necessarily want to be rich." On this topic his voice would always become very sad, with traces of bitterness.

Viola sorely wanted to support Albert in his business ventures, but she couldn't help wondering how he and Bob Haines could ever hope to achieve anything with all the irons they had in the fire. She and Albert talked about that all the time. He could be so nerve-racking at times. Sometimes she wanted to scream.

Turning from discussing the McDonald's franchise at the airport, she said to Albert with resignation, “I'll start dinner in a few minutes. I'm preaching at Rev. Crawford's church tonight. Are you coming?”

“No, I can't. I've a Kiwanis meeting tonight,” he said, looking at his wristwatch.

That was another thing that bugged her. Albert’s churchgoing had dropped off considerably since he started running around with his born-again friends.

Chapter Eight

After dinner Rev. Flowers went into her study to take a load off her feet before getting ready for church later. She sat down in her favorite chair, her father's old rocking chair. Often when relaxing she would sit in that chair and watch the birds come and go from the bird feeder in their back yard. It was the same rocking chair that her father used to sit in years ago when studying his Bible when they lived in Iowa where he had his church.

When a child she loved sitting on the floor at his feet reading her kiddie books while he read his Bible. She loved it when he would reach down without looking up from his Bible, pat her reassuringly on the head, and praise her studiousness. "Remember, honey, that most of the important secrets of the world are locked up in books," he would tell the precocious five-year-old. "Especially this one," he would add, fondly cuddling his Bible. Sometimes he would lift her up and place her gently on his lap and read portions of the Bible to her. It always amazed him how much of it she comprehended.

"I don't know why that surprises you, Tom. You know how smart Viola is in Sunday school," his wife would say proudly about their small daughter.

Rev. Flowers' father was a gentle, soft-spoken man with a quiet dignity many people often mistook for weakness, sometimes even his own wife. "Elder Henry was out of line taking over the finance committee meeting like he did this afternoon, Tom. You should've called him on it. You appointed Elder Smith to be in charge of that committee, not Elder Henry," was typical of the kinds of critical remarks his wife would make to him from time to time. "It's all right, dear. Everything turned out fine," he answered softly that day.

To his wife he had missed the point. He should have taken control of the meeting. His reticence often encouraged bullies in the church to challenge his authority. Viola's grandfather, the late

Bishop T. J. Crombie, founded and headed the Church of God & Spirit until his death. The Church of God & Spirit was a national church with branches all over the United States, especially in the South and Midwest. When Viola's grandfather died, leadership of the national church passed to her father, who nearly lost control of the church to some dissidents who thought he was too weak to hold on to it. Even though Rev. Flowers loved her father dearly and admired him very much, she too at times saw his gentleness as a weakness.

Though she had many of the kinder traits of her father, particularly his gentleness and his love of people, Rev. Flowers also had important traits of her grandfather, particularly his strength and political cunning. While her father was an unassuming man who more resembled a mild-mannered poet than a gospel preacher, her grandfather was a large, imposing black man with a deep booming voice, whose commanding presence caused people to give him their undivided attention. Whereas her father ruled the national church by consensus and was masterful at getting people to agree on things, her grandfather ruled the church by virtue of his mighty personality. He ruled the national church with an iron fist. Unlike her father who didn't stand out much in a crowd, her powerful grandfather dwarfed everything around him.

She admired how her grandfather had built the national church from scratch when he broke off from the Church of God in Christ decades ago, taking a few other disaffected churches with him. He reorganized the breakaway churches into the Church of God & Spirit, which he then headed. Although her grandfather died before she was born, he was her hero. She kept a large framed photograph of him in her study on the wall next to a picture of Jesus. It was comforting having her two most favorite people looking down on her, looking after her as she sat at her desk every day. She strove hard to be like them. In things spiritual she would look up and talk to Jesus, but in matters ministerial, she would look up and speak to her grandfather.

"What would you do, Grandpa?" she would ask the stern-faced black man in the photograph whenever she had a difficult church problem that was giving her trouble. Her grandfather, with his broad square chin, his wide flat nose, and his steely dark eyes, always provided a sound answer.

She got up, stretched, and went to her computer to check her e-mail.

Chapter Nine

When a small girl Viola loved going down South with her father to visit Aunt Belle who was then living in Florenceville, Georgia. Aunt Belle was her grandfather's sister. Lettie was too young to remember those trips. Viola remembered Aunt Belle's old wood-burning cooking stove in the kitchen that always had something boiling on top or something delicious baking in the oven. She remembered the nutmeg grater that Aunt Belle kept hanging beside the stove to spice up the pies and puddings that she was always making. She remembered the times when she went hiking with Aunt Belle along the dirt roads and railroad tracks looking for wild berries. On one such hiking trip Aunt Belle suddenly stopped and took little Viola by the arm and carefully guided her away from a promising looking patch of berries.

"Don't go in those bushy weeds, child. There're probably snakes in there." She pointed to some dragonflies flying amid the dewberries. "Down here in Georgia these dragonflies are called 'snake doctors' because snakes eat them for medicine," she told little Viola, frightening her so much that she didn't want to pick anymore wild fruit and berries.

Little Viola enjoyed listening to Aunt Belle talk about her father when he was a small boy. "That boy was always getting into mischief. Tom used to beat Little Tom with his razor strop until that child had welts on his legs so bad that he could barely walk." The "Tom" Aunt Belle was talking about was her big brother (Viola and Lettie's grandfather) before he became an important bishop of his church. "Little Tom" was her nephew, Viola and Lettie's father.

"Grandpa used to whip Daddy when he was a little boy?" little Viola asked with big eyes. This was the first time she had heard that story, and found it unbelievable because their father never spanked them.

“Tom was very strict on your father, sometimes a little too strict. He was deathly afraid that Little Tom would get into trouble with the law. The law was very hard on black folks in those days, especially the males,” Aunt Belle explained.

Talking about the law always seemed to make Aunt Belle very nervous, Viola recalled, which was quite strange since Aunt Belle wasn't afraid of white people. Viola remembered a particular time when she went shopping in town with Aunt Belle who lived on the outskirts of Florenceville. That was the day when Aunt Belle excoriated a white teenage clerk in a drugstore they had entered to buy themselves ice-cream cones. After requiring them to wait until all the white children were served first, even those who came into the drugstore after them, the young white female clerk finally began serving them their ice-cream cones. While scooping the ice-cream she looked up and saw little Viola hugging a doll she had taken down from the rack.

“Put that down! I should make you buy it now! Nobody'll want that doll now that you've had your black hands on it!” the young clerk screamed at little Viola, causing her to cry.

Aunt Belle was furious. Her eyes blazing, her index finger wagging, she exclaimed to the young white clerk, “You apologize to that child, or else I'll come behind that counter and teach you a lesson you'll never forget!” The white teenager's eyes inflated like balloons. She had never been spoken to like that before by a black person. Other white customers in the drugstore looked on in disbelief.

"I said apologize!” Aunt Belle demanded as she moved to go around the counter.

Terrified, the young clerk looked at Aunt Belle, and at the other white people watching to see what she was going to do, then broke into tears and fled to the office in the back. The owner rushed out to see what had happened, but when he saw who the angry black woman was, his fleshy white face relaxed. Aunt Belle, a nurse, was a longtime customer who over the years had sent him many of her patients with their prescriptions.

“Is something wrong, Belle?” he asked her politely.

"You should teach your employees how to treat your customers properly," she upbraided him for what had just happened.

He apologized for his young clerk, explaining that she was a new employee. He offered little Viola the doll as a gift from the store.

The child gladly took it.

"No. I'll pay for it, Mr. Finley," Aunt Belle insisted, referring to the doll. She opened her big black pocketbook and handed him some money. "And don't forget to take out for our ice-cream cones," she added. After receiving her change, she took little Viola by the hand and left the drug store.

Because Aunt Belle had attended high school for awhile in the North where she took a Red Cross first-aid course, she was the closest thing in that part of rural Georgia that black folks had as a doctor or nurse. Since the nearest hospital was nearly fifty miles away, and because the one white doctor in the area wouldn't take black patients, black folks in the area looked to her for their health care needs. With her herbs, home remedies, medical books, and the little bit of real medicine that she remembered from her Red Cross training, Aunt Belle tried to help them the best she could, and she even made a modest living at it. Even some poor whites came to her with their ailments.

Over time she became a highly regarded licensed county nurse.

Rev. Flowers loved her Aunt Belle and thought she was one of the proudest persons she had ever known. When she died, Aunt Belle was bedridden in a nursing home, hardly able to recognize people's face. It was very sad, Viola thought, because Aunt Belle had lived such an active and interesting life.

Chapter Ten

"Good morning, Rev. Flowers," a male voice said from the doorway of her office at the church. She looked up from her desk and saw a familiar figure in the archway with bright sunlight washing over him from behind. "C'mon in, Rev. Mike. How are you today?" she said, putting her pen down and smiling a broad welcoming smile.

A pudgy, shabbily dressed white man shuffled over and took a seat. He had a fresh sugary doughnut in one hand and a Dixie Cup of hot coffee in the other, both of which he had just gotten from Beulah in the church kitchen. Beulah was the church cook. Rev. Mike was a regular visitor who knew his way around the church. He put his coffee down next to him and ate his doughnut, carefully so not to spill any crumbs.

"Jesus has done it again. What a beautiful day," he said reverently, looking out at the beautiful California sky.

"Indeed he has. God's love is everywhere on this lovely morning. Did you notice the little baby doves running around in the courtyard? When I came in this morning, the mother dove was standing by so quietly in the grass that I nearly stepped on one of her chicks. I guess she was teaching them how to fly," Rev. Flowers smiled.

The white man suddenly became very quiet. Rev. Flowers broadened her smile and went back to work. From time to time Rev. Mike dropped by just to sit and visit for awhile, often dozing off in the chair. Thus it wasn't surprising that she soon heard him snoring. She wondered when he last had a good night's sleep.

Rev. Mike claimed he was an ordained minister and had what he called an "open air" ministry. "Doing the Lord's work out in the fresh air," he would say when describing his religious work. At first the church's cook Beulah believed he was nothing but a crazy homeless white person.

“He sleeps in his car, Rev. Flowers. He's no ordained minister. He ain't got no church. My husband saw him one morning with his shirt off washing himself up under the viaduct,” Beulah said when he first started coming to the church offering to do odd jobs for a little loose change or a meal. Eventually Beulah got to know him and now she liked him. Last week he fixed the leaky pipe under the church sink in exchange for some turnip greens and ham hocks. “But I still don't think he's no preacher. He's a nice man, though, even if he’s a little touched in the head,” Beulah said to Rev. Flowers one day.

Rev. Flowers wasn't sure Beulah was right about Rev. Mike. After all, she thought, Jesus was a carpenter with an outdoors ministry who traveled around the countryside, barefooted and in rags, delivering the word of God. The people along Jesus’ route probably thought he was just a crazy bum muttering foolish things. She often wondered how Jesus would fare today if he came down and walked the streets of modern-day America, whilst talking about helping the poor and freeing the oppressed. Didn’t long ago the rich and powerful kill him for doing that? Therefore she disagreed with Beulah about Rev. Mike's being nothing but a bum.

Although she didn't really know much about Rev. Mike—such as where he lived, how he managed income-wise, or who his family was, assuming he had one, or even what his last name was—Rev. Flowers knew that he sometimes visited inmates in jail and sick people in the hospitals. She had seen him there a few times when she was making her rounds. She also knew that he regularly visited the various churches in the area, and if the church had a soup kitchen, he would collect the leftover food that would otherwise go into the garbage, and take it off somewhere. The speculation was that he served that food to the poor.

But churches couldn't save leftovers for him on a regular basis, because they never knew when he would show up. He was such an unreliable fellow. Sometimes he wouldn't stop by for months at a time. He would just disappear for long periods of time. No one knew his telephone number (if he had a phone) or a location where he could be reached, so regrettably whatever food churches had left over from their soup kitchens at the end of the day usually had to be thrown away.

The same was true of the handyman work he would do for you with the tools he kept in his old jalopy. Because you never knew when Rev. Mike would drop by, you couldn't depend on him to do work for you. This was a pity since he was a pretty good plumber and carpenter who gladly accepted whatever gratuity you gave him.

When he finished fixing something for them, Rev. Flowers would say to him, "I realize that you don't want to be paid for doing God's work, but here's a little something to help with the expenses of your ministry," and she would pay him what she felt the job was worth. He would thank her and pocket the money without even counting it. If Rev. Flowers wasn't around anywhere on the premises, Beulah would pay him with a big meal.

Rev. Mike's open-air ministry reminded Rev. Flowers of her good friend Rev. Brooks' children AIDS ministry. To her, both men were Christian pastors serving God in different ways.

Rev. Mike started dropping by the church about five years ago. Early one morning while working in her office, Rev. Flowers sensed that someone was behind her. She turned around with a start, and there he was, standing in her open doorway. The strange white man frightened her at first. She figured he was a homeless person who had wandered in off the street. Then as now there was much homelessness in Los Angeles.

In fact, a few years ago for a short while she allowed homeless people to sleep in her church at night and use the restrooms during the day. It pained her to think of anyone having to sleep on the streets, particularly children. The word spread quickly in the local homeless community, and soon her church was overflowing every night with homeless people seeking shelter. They brought their shopping carts, cardboard boxes and tents. Those who couldn't find space in the church slept in the church's courtyard. In the morning the church and the courtyard were a mess. Garbage and trash were everywhere. Even worse, many of the homeless started leaving their shopping carts and possessions at the church during the day while they roamed the streets for food and the other things they needed to stay alive.

Church parishioners began complaining vehemently, wanting to throw the homeless out. "It's gotten so bad, Rev. Flowers, that our members are afraid to come to church at night. What's more, the church has begun to stink. I think they're urinating and shitting out in the courtyard," one irate parishioner said, exaggerating greatly as she handed Rev. Flowers a petition signed by over a hundred church members demanding that the homeless be kept from trespassing.

The question: "Would kicking them out be unchristian?" troubled Rev. Flowers deeply. She had no doubt that letting the homeless sleep in the church at night was the Christian thing to do. After all, the space on most nights wasn't being used during those hours. She was sure it was what the Lord wanted the church to do. But was their Christian charity overwhelming the church? Was the problem too big for them? Had they bitten off more than they could chew? For the first time she was struck by the Sisyphean nature of the undertaking. She thought of how whole sections of downtown Los Angeles turned into Hoovervilles at night. She knew the homeless problem had overwhelmed many other cities as well. "The intractable homeless problem," one cynic called it. What an awful dilemma this posed for Rev. Flowers.

That night she got down on her knees and prayed for wisdom. "What should we do, Dear Lord? Those poor people have no place to go. Many are women and children. It seems that no one wants them around. That no one cares about them. We just had a long presidential campaign, and not a single word was said about the millions of homeless in this country. Neither by the Republicans nor the Democrats. Our recent mayoral race wasn't much better. Don't our political leaders care? We tried to do something about the problem ourselves, but we too failed. Please, O Lord, tell me what to do. I beseech you," she begged God with tears in her eyes.

That night a solution came to her in her sleep, and bright and early the next morning she went over to the church, woke up all the homeless people in the church and courtyard, and had a meeting with them. She frankly told them about the problem that the trustee board and the members of the church had with their being there. "What would you do if you were in our shoes?" she asked them earnestly, her heart heavy.

They appreciated her predicament.

An old homeless woman agreed that letting them sleep in the church at night didn't seem to be working out, but she had a suggestion. "It would help us a lot, Rev. Flowers, if we could get a good hot meal every once in awhile, especially the children." She was thinking of the church's nice stainless steel kitchen that in her opinion was being underutilized. The woman was with her three small grandchildren who had to join her on the streets when their mother and sole provider was imprisoned on drug charges.

A man asked about the church at least letting them use the toilets on some kind of regular basis. "We can go back to sleeping on the streets easy enough, Rev. Flowers, but do you know how awful it is to have to take a crap and nobody'll let you use their toilet. Most gas stations these days only let their customers use their toilets," the man said sadly. Rev. Flowers later learned that a Main Street restaurant proprietor had recently beaten that man up for taking a leak against the restaurant building. Another man in his early thirties complained about how hard it was for him to get ready for work every morning.

"Everyday I'm terrified that people at work will think I stink," he said unhappily.

"Work every morning?" Rev. Flowers moaned to herself, her eyes wide. She was surprised to learn that many of them had jobs. This shocking revelation was so contrary to the popular notion of the homeless portrayed by the media, she thought. Most of the homeless using the church were women and children, not just black men, and some of them were white people.

Rev. Flowers suggested they form a committee among themselves of people who could sit down with her and other church officials to come up with a list of things the church could do to help them. That is, what the church could do to help them other than letting them sleep there. The old lady with the grandchildren was the first to volunteer to serve on that committee. Representatives of the homeless and the church held meetings and agreed to a plan that the board of trustees and the church membership later approved.

Among other things, the church agreed to expand its hot meals programs to include sit-down meals for the homeless in the church dining room. The homeless women were particularly grateful for the breakfasts for the children. Furthermore, because the homeless children needed decent clothes for school, the church began distributing used clothing and shoes to the homeless collected from church members and the community, an idea that eventually led to the church's opening its own thrift shop in a storefront a couple of blocks from the church. The church also approved opening their toilets and showers to the homeless, provided they signed in first before picking up the key. No smoking, drugs or alcohol would be tolerated on the premises.

Finally, because Rev. Flowers couldn't bear seeing them leave the mess hall in the evenings with no place to sleep, especially the beautiful little children, the church started calling around and finding space every night in the various city shelters for those who wanted beds for the night. Thus every evening after supper the church bus took them to various city shelters, even picking them up in the mornings and bringing them back to the church for breakfast. Some church members started opening up their homes at night to the homeless.

The church's homeless program was a great success. It ended up providing some jobs for the homeless themselves. The grandmother with the three small grandchildren, in fact, became a full-time salaried employee of the church helping the cook Beulah in the kitchen.

It was now after eight a.m. and Rev. Mike was still in the armchair snoring.

"Who am I to question God's assignments," Rev. Flowers said to herself as she tiptoed quietly from the room so as not to awaken him. She knew Beulah would feed him breakfast when he woke up.

Chapter Eleven

Albert considered the day he first met Bob Haines and his other new white Christian friends the luckiest day of his life. It was at a social during an evangelical conference that he and Viola had attended in Hawthorne, a small city a few miles south of Los Angeles. The people there were mostly white born-again Christians. At the social, the men of the group, including Albert Flowers, gathered outside for smokes, where they talked a lot about entrepreneurship. Most of them owned or aspired to own their own businesses. Albert was amazed when one of the white men turned to him in a friendly way and asked matter-of-factly,

"What line of business are you in, Al?" Albert was in hog heaven. He had found his tribe. Here was a group of men who thought like he did on most issues, and among those guys, having one's own business was the natural order of things. Because he was there, everyone just assumed he was a businessman also.

Another thing, with his new conservative friends, unlike when around his white liberal and progressive friends, his race seemed immaterial. All that mattered to them was that he too loved making money, and that seemed to be enough. What a rare, wonderful experience for a black man! Albert Flowers was so happy that he was nearly moved to tears. He had found his real home. A place where he didn't have to be ashamed of his love for business. He was now among men who appreciated the excitement of putting together a business plan and watching the business move towards success. They were men with whom he could share his dreams. Men who knew what a bottom line was.

Albert saw them as men who were brave, strong and determined, all qualities he admired in people. A few of them had gone through bankruptcy, not once but several times, and unfazed many were starting over in business again.

"While sitting there in bankruptcy court waiting for my case to be called, I thought of this great new idea to get back into business.

I couldn't wait to be declared bankrupt so I could get back into action again. This time, though, I decided to keep my in-laws out of it. It was my goddamn brother-in-law who ruined my last business. I shouldn't have listened to my wife when she begged me to put him in charge of sales. That four-flusher even gave me a phony resume. Can you imagine that, my own brother-in-law. When that lazy bastard should've been out on the road taking care of business, he'd be holed up in a bar somewhere getting smash. I should've fired the sonofabitch the first week I hired him," one of Albert's new friends said about a new business he was planning.

He even had his new investment capital all lined up.

Those men were why Albert became a Republican. He now often reflected back with regret why he remained a Democrat for as long as he did. He was definitely convinced that white Republicans, unlike white liberals and progressives, didn't mind if a black man made a little money for himself, and they would accept you if you showed some get-up-and-go about yourself.

He later went into business with a couple of those white men, but their business failed. Albert learned a lot from that experience. Then he tried again with another white partner, this time with Bob Haines and their shuttle van business.

Chapter Twelve

For months Rev. Brooks, the young black pastor from New Berry Baptist Church, had been telling Rev. Flowers about the AIDS children he had been seeing in the hospital. Most of them were born from crack mothers. "I've made working with those poor children a big part of my ministry. The Lord woke me up early one morning and gave me this important mission," he told Rev. Flowers the first time they talked about the plight of HIV/AIDS in the African American community. What she learned about AIDS from Rev. Brooks astounded her, and her startled face showed it. So he invited her to accompany him to the hospital sometime to visit the sick children. "They can use all the prayers they can get," he said.

She accepted his invitation, and in his car on their way to the hospital Rev. Brooks said, "Vi, the Black Church has to become more involved in the fight against HIV/AIDS. We black clergy sit passively by with our heads in the sand while this awful disease devastates our community. We must take action. What are we afraid of?"

His remark about the black clergy's not speaking out on AIDS hit a sore spot with Rev. Flowers, who knew deep in her heart that she was one of the black preachers he was talking about. Like many black ministers, she too had refused to think about the HIV/AIDS problem in the black community. To her and many of her black colleagues, AIDS was a gay disease that gays had brought on themselves. Men having sex with men was against the laws of nature as well as against the will of God, they believed. Just a couple of Sundays ago she preached a sermon on the topic.

So she told Rev. Brooks the truth about how she felt about the matter, which shocked him.

"I'm surprised at you, Vi. You're the last person I would've thought would be homophobic. You always taught us in church that it was wrong to be prejudiced," he retorted in utter disbelief.

What Rev. Brooks meant was that when a small boy going to her church, he attended Sunday school faithfully and was one of her best pupils. Then his parents suddenly broke up and divorced, and he and his mother and siblings then moved out of town. For a long time Rev. Flowers lost track of them. One day some years later Rev. Flowers ran into him at the Fox Hills Mall. He was now an ordained minister working in Los Angeles. He told her that day, "You've been an important influence in my life. You're the reason I became a minister. You showed me how much good work a person of God can do in the community."

Highly flattered by what he just told her, Rev. Flowers replied, "Just call me Vi, Reggie. We're colleagues now, not teacher and pupil." When explaining to her why he changed his denomination and why he was now a Baptist, Rev. Brooks said, "You always taught us to think for ourselves, and to find God in our own way. So I decided the Baptist Church was the best church for me."

That was a few years ago; now they were the best of friends.

"I'm not prejudiced against gays, Reggie," she said, "I only disapprove of their unnatural life style. In fact I'm presently counseling a couple of young gay members of my church who desperately want to change their ways. They want to be good Christians again."

"Unnatural, Vi?" Rev. Brooks said, looking at her askance. "At least a tenth of the human race is homosexual and God made them like that. Doesn't that count for something? Are you questioning God's handiwork? I guess on this subject you and I read the Bible differently."

"I guess we do," she said coldly, glad to move the conversation back to the AIDS children that was less controversial. She could see from Rev. Brooks' crestfallen face that she had disappointed him immensely.

That morning what she saw on her maiden hospital tour of the children's AIDS ward was heartrending. Small children fighting to stay alive because of their diseased little bodies. They reminded her of the starving children of Africa sometimes seen in news magazines. Those big moony eyes sunk deeply into those bony little faces. Those little bodies that were nothing but skin and bones. Those beseeching eyes that grabbed your heart like small fists when looking at you.

The strong pull of a particular pair of eyes caused Rev. Flowers to turn, and across the room she saw a little girl eyeing her. There was something so sad and pleading about those big pitiful eyes that she had to go over to the little girl, who was about four or five years old. It was hard to tell her age because of her withered condition.

Rev. Brooks joined her at the little girl's bedside. The child reached up and took Rev. Flowers' hand and squeezed it tightly like she didn't want to let her go. In her delirium the little girl must have thought that Rev. Flowers was her mother who had died of AIDS months ago. Maybe she confused Rev. Flowers with another relative she loved. Or maybe the little girl just needed some human warmth.

Whatever the case, she wouldn't let go of Rev. Flowers' hand, holding it as if her life depended on it. This brought tears to Rev. Flowers' eyes. She wondered about the mother. What kind of person would do this to her own child?

She remembered reading about a criminal prosecutor in Texas who was charging AIDS mothers with murder when their children died from AIDS. When she first read that in the newspaper, she thought what that Texas district attorney was doing was cruel and heartless. But now standing there watching that beautiful little child suffer so, she wasn't so sure that charging those mothers criminally was wrong. Standing there she found herself not only hating the disease of AIDS, but also hating the mothers who had passed the disease to their children.

She hated their selfish and reckless behavior. Crack addicts, prostitutes, and young promiscuous hussies in lipstick and high heels came to mind, and it disgusted her. Then she caught herself and felt ashamed of herself for having all that unchristian bitterness. She silently asked God for forgiveness. She asked him for the wisdom to better understand the awful problem, and she begged him for the compassion to deal with it.

She recalled one Sunday seeing from the pulpit a sickly looking, disheveled young woman come in during the service and take a seat in the back near the door. Was that poor woman a drug addict seeking help? To her credit Rev. Flowers did try to help her, but by the time she got back to the woman after the service was over, she was gone. Now Rev. Flowers wondered if that woman was pregnant and had AIDS at the time. The very thought made her shudder.

The little girl continued to hold her hand tightly.

"You go ahead and make your rounds, Reggie. I'll stay here with her. I think she needs me," she told Rev. Brooks as she sat down at bedside and held the little girl's hand. About an hour later, the child fell asleep sucking her other thumb and the sight touched Rev. Flowers deeply.

On their way home Rev. Brooks told her that the little girl was typical of the many children living with AIDS at the hospital. "Most are African American," he said, "Sometimes their suffering pains you so much that you want to just throw your Bible down and run out of there. Get away from them as far as you can. Then one of them will smile at you, and you realize there's no other place in the world where you would rather be. No other place where God wants you to be."

She then learned something from Rev. Brooks that made her feel much better. Something that helped her clear up some troubling notions she had about AIDS.

"It's a misconception, Vi, that female crack addicts and prostitutes are mainly responsible for the ravages of AIDS in the black community. While it's true that drug addiction and prostitution deserve some of the blame for HIV and AIDS in our community, unfaithful husbands and boyfriends are mainly responsible for so many women getting the disease. We black men just have to do a better job of keeping our peckers in our pants," Rev. Brooks said frankly before realizing to whom he was speaking. He then said sheepishly, "Please excuse my language, Vi, but I didn't know any other way to put it."

Rev. Flowers was glad that he had so colorfully described the problem. The following Sunday she delivered a sermon on the need to fight AIDS in the black community, which she called: "Don't Poison The Water In Your Own Well." She told of a man in biblical times who stole things from his neighbors and hid them down in his drinking well. The man ended up unwittingly poisoning himself and his entire family, including his children.

"You black family men must do a better job of staying home at night and not bringing home things that will harm your wife and children. And you young single men must do a better job of keeping your tools in the shed at night," she euphemistically told her congregation that Sunday. This was the first time she had dared to touch the topic. In fact, this was the first time she had acknowledged the problem publicly.

From all the "Amens" from the women, plus all the embarrassed looks from the men, everyone apparently got her point.

****

One afternoon when Rev. Flowers returned to the parsonage after spending the afternoon at the hospital with the little girl, she had a long honest talk with God. She was very angry. And in her anger she questioned God why he had seemingly abandoned the sick girl. "Why O Lord did you let her get AIDS? What did she do to deserve that? I can understand why you would punish gays, drug addicts and prostitutes, but why innocent children?" she asked him with tears in her eyes, her fists clenched.

When God answered none of her questions, she took his silence as a rebuke. So she humbly asked for forgiveness. "I'm sorry, Father. Please excuse my impertinence. I'm just a lowly servant of yours seeking more information so I can better serve thee. So please forgive me." Then she asked meekly in almost a whisper, "Lord, would I be stepping over the line if I asked: 'Why don't you cure her? You have the power. She's just an innocent child who's done nothing wrong.'" Still no answer.

Large gray clouds from the Pacific Ocean darkened the sky.

With tears welling in her eyes, Viola Flowers asked God another very strange question. She just couldn't help herself. "Are you doing this to us because we're black?" she asked with the innocence of a small child. She sounded like the little children who had asked her that same question one afternoon after church. That pitiable question that might have been the selfsame question that their ancestors had asked centuries ago while stumbling aboard slave ships in chains.

When God still refused to answer any of her questions, she beseeched him, sobbing, "Please, God, please help me understand. Help me put an end to all this doubting I'm suffering. All the confusion. Please give me the strength to accept your will unquestionably."

There was still no answer.

Later that night when alone in her study she dropped to her knees and spoke to God again. She had to. Her life now wasn't making any sense. "Please, Lord, what did those poor little hospitalized children do to deserve this? Why have you forsaken them? Aren't they your children too? Don't you love them?" she asked, almost begging him for a reply.

All her life Viola Flowers had loved the Lord, obeyed him, and faithfully served him, and now he was playing games with her. He was now no better than some crooked shell-game operator hustling on some street corner, she thought with bitterness. "Damn you!" she cursed God scathingly about the little girl. Then she crumbled to the floor in little pieces.

After lying there for awhile, ashamed of herself, she got on her knees again and begged forgiveness.

Chapter Thirteen

Rev. Flowers decided she would attend Rev. Brooks' big ministerial meeting on HIV/AIDS at Reggie's church, and on the night of the meeting she took a seat in a pew near the door so she could leave early if she wished. She had come to the meeting only out of curiosity. Last week her good friend Rev. Reggie Brooks came to her with a public service announcement that he said was very important that he wanted aired on her weekly radio show. Something that started as a hobby, Rev. Flowers hosted a local radio show that featured gospel music and on-air prayers for the sick and shut-ins.

The notice, Viola Flowers discovered when she read it, was an urgent call to all black clergymen in the city to meet about dealing with a monumental public health problem that threatened to wipe out the black community. "This is the gravest crisis we African Americans have faced since slavery," the notice read, which called for a meeting at Rev. Brooks' New Berry Baptist Church. It gave the date, time and address. Although the notice didn't say what the public health problem was, she knew it had to be AIDS because helping AIDS children had become Rev. Brook's life. He and she had discussed the subject often, and he was the one who told her about how AIDS was also ravishing the continent of Africa. She had read the same thing about Africa in some newspaper or magazine, but hadn't believed it.

When Rev. Brooks brought the notice to the radio station, he didn't ask Rev. Flowers for special treatment. He merely asked that it be included with all her other public service announcements for the week. Yet for some reason she set Rev. Brooks' notice aside from the other announcements and read it separately before every commercial break, increasing her ardor with each reading. Not only did she read the announcement on her own radio show, on her own initiative she contacted other religious radio and television programs in Los Angeles and had it read there as well. She knew how important the meeting was to Reggie, and she wanted to help him get the word out.

Then in spite of her misgivings about getting involved in the HIV/AIDS issue, she ended up attending the meeting. She didn't know why, she just did. She was leery of the meeting because homosexuals might be involved. She recalled what a fellow black pastor said a couple of weeks ago when she told him about the splendid job Rev. Brooks was doing with his "Help the AIDS Children" program.

Rev. Owens scratched his head and frowned. “Rev. Flowers, I just don't know about Brother Brooks. Some folks are saying he's a ‘down-low’ boy himself,” he said scornfully, totally ignoring the merits of Reggie’s children program. That irked her tremendously, but she let the remark pass without comment. She was mindful of the cruel remarks that Jesus often suffered, along with the sticks and stones, when moving among the people doing God's work. “God's disciples must have callused feet because of the many jagged rocks they’ll have to cross on their travels,” she recalled her minister father saying once.

At the time of her conversation with Rev. Owens she didn't exactly know what "down-low" meant, except she knew it wasn't flattering. (She later learned that a "down-low" person was a male, often a married man with a family, who had sex with other males on the q.t.) She dismissed Rev. Owens’ disparaging remark about Rev. Brooks as just another instance of clerical envy. Because Rev. Reggie Brooks was a young minister, many of the older black preachers resented his rapid rise in the local black clergy.

It wasn't that Rev. Brooks saw himself as a civil rights or political leader of the black people, for he didn't. He hated the limelight. It was just that he was often called upon to speak on AIDS issues due to his involvement with the AIDS children. Being so visible and vocal on radio and television had begun to earn him a few enemies amid black preachers whose territory he was thought to be threatening. Some older black ministers were envious of the success of Rev. Brooks’ small Baptist church that was growing by leaps and bounds, particularly with young people.

"Reggie, I think the way you brought that church back to life is just short of miraculous," Rev. Flowers congratulated him once on the good job he was doing with his first church. Down to only a dozen or so members, New Berry Baptist Church was nearly dead when Rev. Brooks took it over.

"Now you have one of the largest Sunday schools in the city. How did you do it?" she asked, feeling a little envy herself since her Sunday school attendance had leveled off and it seemed that nothing she did helped to improve the situation. She believed that a healthy Sunday school was vital to a healthy church.

The answer to Rev. Flowers' question was simple. Because Rev. Brooks opened his church up to the kinds of music that the youth enjoyed, the attendance of young people at his church grew at a phenomenal rate. The open-mike sessions on Youth Night on Wednesdays were so popular that young musical groups—hip hop, R & B, gospel and pop—came from all over Los Angeles to participate in the church's musical workshops and amateur hours.

And the church had one of the finest recording studios of its kind in the city where the kids could make demos of their songs. Important people from the record companies often attended the Wednesday night sessions where every unused room and out-of-the-way space in the church was packed with young people warming up or rehearsing their numbers.

When Rev. Reggie Brooks graduated from the seminary and became an ordained minister, he came to Rev. Flowers often for advice on how to be more effective in his ministry. He saw her as one of his mentors. In fact she was his main role model. She told him frankly about the ins and outs of pastoring a church.

"Go slow at first, especially when contemplating changes. Study the lay of the land first. Get to know your members. Identify the church leaders. Not just the ones who think they're the leaders, but the ones who are really the leaders. Learn who your supporters are. Learn who the difficult church members are. Try to win them over if you can, but stick to your guns. Bend if you must, but don't show weakness. Beware of the politics that will be there waiting for you. Trust me, Reggie, there will be politics there, even if not visible on the surface. And by all means, always watch your back. Identify the members you can depend on in tough times," she advised the young pastor.

Those were all things her grandfather had taught her father, which her father taught her. Things that weren't taught in the seminary.

"You make it sound like going into war," Rev. Brooks laughed.

She smiled and said, "I didn't mean to sound Machiavellian, but I watched my father struggled for years to keep control of our national church. I was appalled at all the backbiting and skullduggery I saw. And I've had my own internal fights over the years."

Rev. Brooks' public announcement was very effective. Black preachers from all over the city, of all faiths and denominations, began flocking into the small Baptist church. "Reggie did a good job of spreading word of the meeting," Rev. Flowers said to herself as she sat there waiting for things to get underway.

She gave a friendly wave to some ministers she hadn't seen in years. Most of the leading black ministers in the city were there. She was particularly pleased to see Bishop Benjamin Z. Neely. If there was one person Rev. Brooks would need onboard for the success of his cause, Bishop Neely was that person, she thought. Bishop Neely was the most highly respected black clergyman in the city. His involvement with social justice and community causes, to say nothing of political matters, went way back to the Civil Rights days when he not only counseled the great Rev. Martin Luther King, Jr., but marched with him as well.

A large handsome man now in his eighties, Bishop Neely was one of the elder statesmen of the black clergy, not just in Los Angeles, but nationally. He had come to the meeting with Rev. Brewer of the A.M.E. Church. The small auditorium was full; there were even a few white ministers present, including a Catholic priest.

"Reggie's done a fine job," Rev. Flowers said to herself again.

She said hello to Rev. Bell, the minister who married her and Albert some years ago. He was with two preachers she didn't know. Rev. Bell's being there caused her to reminisce about her marriage. When Albert asked her to marry him, she had been seeing him for less than six months. It was "seeing" rather than "dating" because that's really what their relationship was in the beginning. They were more like good friends who occasionally went out and did fun things together, nothing physical, albeit she had to slap Albert's hands away a few times. A good friend had introduced her to Albert after she and Manny Scott broke up.

"He's a good catch, Viola. He has a good-paying job with the county, and he's a high official with the employee's union. Most of all, he's a good church-going man," the friend told her, who had exaggerated a bit since Albert was only the assistant treasurer of his union at the time.

She met Albert Flowers and liked him. He was a chunkily built man with large hands, a round pleasant face, and a big bright politician's smile. Most important, he seemed to have a good heart. It didn't matter to her that he wasn't exactly good-looking, because since Manny Scott she didn't trust good-looking men anymore. After Manny Scott she saw handsome men as dangerous Venus Fly Traps whose beautiful pedals were only there to attract prey. Everything about her relationship with Manny Scott had been extra intense—their times alone, their times out together, their deep intellectual discussions, especially on theology, their arguments, their awful fights, and their passionate lovemaking.

Therefore, when she and Rev. Scott broke up, meeting a nice, easy-going teddy bear like Albert Flowers was a welcome change. Fun-loving, Albert always made her laugh, whereas Manny always made her cry. What impressed her most about Albert was his large ambition. She saw him as a man who wanted to do something with his life. He wasn't full of crap like Manny.

"Is anyone sitting here?" a young attractive black woman asked Rev. Flowers, jarring her from her mental wandering. The woman pointed to the empty seat next to her. The church was now nearly full.

“No. Let me move my things.” Vi picked up her shoulder bag and stood so the woman could get past her.

“I'm Rev. Bowman from the Calvary Baptist Church,” the woman introduced herself.

“I'm Rev. Viola Flowers from the Church of God & Spirit.”

“Are you *the* Rev. Flowers on the radio? Oh my! I listen to you every Sunday,” the woman said excitedly, making Viola feel like a celebrity.

Rev. Flowers was glad to see another woman minister at the meeting. It pleased her very much that everyday more young women were entering the ministry. It angered her that there were still black churches that didn't allow women ministers in their order. The "women question" was one of the reasons her grandfather broke with the Church of Christ years ago. While supporting the Church of Christ's basic trinitarianism of the infallibility of Scripture, the need for regeneration, and the baptism of the Holy Ghost, he and the ministers who left with him also believed in the sanctification and ordination of women. The Church of Christ didn't.

“Limiting the role of women in the church is a lot of nonsense,” her grandfather said when he cut all ties with the Church of Christ, a holiness church preferred by many African Americans at the time. “My mother ran our little church and preached every Sunday for nearly twenty years before we finally got another male pastor,” he said, “So I know what women can do, and so does God.”

Up on the dais alone, Rev. Brooks opened the meeting with a prayer, and then explained why they were assembled. He did a good job presenting the problem, Rev. Flowers thought. She hadn't realized the extent that HIV/AIDS had beset the black community, particularly among the young people. The tragic statistics sent cold shivers through her.

As she listened she was even more surprised to learn how rapidly the disease was spreading among heterosexual women. It deeply disturbed her. What Reggie was saying was very serious.

The very foundation of the black community was being threatened by that awful disease, she realized.

From the shock on their faces, many of the other ministers at the meeting had been similarly moved by that information. It was clear to her that African American women were in danger, and that was very alarming. "Going back to the days of slavery, black women have always been the bedrock of the African American people. Even today they are the ones mostly keeping things together in the black community," she had heard Bishop Neely say once.

According to Rev. Brooks, men infected with HIV/AIDS were returning home from prisons in large numbers and infecting their wives and sweethearts, further spreading the disease, which he cited as sufficient reason to distribute condoms in jails and prisons. Many of the ministers at the meeting began to stir uncomfortably when Rev. Brooks left the topic of jails and prisons and began talking about how young people in the community were engaging in unsafe sex and needed condoms as well.

One preacher got to his feet and asked with much irritation, "Don't you have it backwards, Reverend? Shouldn't we be teaching our young people to abstain from sex, not how to have sex?" He looked around for concurrence and found it from the many bobbing heads in the audience. "God warns about premarital sex in the Bible. So shouldn't we be telling the children that having sex before marriage is unchristian?" he added before sitting back down.

"It isn't enough just to teach teenagers abstinence, Rev. Wright," Rev. Brooks answered. "We must teach them safe sexual practices in case they don't abstain. We mustn't put our heads in the sand. There are some young people who'll experiment with sex no matter what we preach on Sundays. These are the ones we must reach with this message."

Many of the ministers were now very nervous, and Rev. Flowers was one of them. Like the others she too felt that some of Reggie's remarks bordered on being outrageous, if not outright blasphemous.

A few preachers got up and left in protest.

Undeterred Rev. Brooks continued, "But the people hit the hardest in our community are our young gay males. Some studies say that in this city one in four black male homosexuals has HIV. That's intolerable. We must act immediately or else our whole community will be wiped out."

Rev. Wright got to his feet again and glared fiercely at the lone black man on stage. "Are you gay, Rev. Brooks?" he fired point-blank at Reggie. A few ministers gasped at the question. There were some nervous snickers.

"I beg your pardon?" Rev. Brooks stammered.

"Are you one of those 'down low' boys? It's a simple question—either yes or no." Rev. Wright was now standing at full height, his face twisted with contempt, and some of the faces around him were also scowling at Rev. Brooks. Some ministers murmured sourly that they too wanted an answer.

Rev. Flowers sat there torn. A part of her sympathized with Reggie, while another part of her also wanted an answer.

Rev. Brooks just stood there stunned; it was like he had just caught a sneaky right cross to the jaw. He should've seen it coming, but he didn't. He should've anticipated such questioning, but he hadn't.

Shaking the cobwebs from his head, he replied, "My sexuality isn't the issue here. The issue here is that we African Americans have a terrible problem in our community that'll destroy us all if we don't act soon. The Black Church must take the lead in doing something about this matter."

"You didn't answered Rev. Wright's question, Rev. Brooks. Do you like boys?" another minister got up and asked, which drew some scattered "amens" amid the preachers.

"Please answer the question, Reggie, please, so we can get on with the meeting," Rev. Flowers begged him silently, her fingers tented mercifully at her lips. She was deeply troubled by the ugly turn the meeting had suddenly taken. Before Rev. Wright's devastating question a few minutes ago, things were going smoothly. All the ministers seemed engaged with what Rev.

Brooks was saying. Now everyone seemed bothered and agitated. Some squirmed in their seats like they were sitting on ants. Others wanted to leave, and a couple of them did get up and depart.

Before Rev. Brooks could answer the question, Bishop Neely got to his feet, causing the church to become quiet and respectful. His powerful presence filled the auditorium. "Brothers and sisters, we've covered a great deal here tonight. Rev. Brooks has given us plenty to think about. We're all getting a little tired and irritable. Why don't we adjourn for tonight and pick it up again at another time."

Thereupon the young female minister sitting next to Rev. Flowers sprung to her feet like a jack-in-the-box and said, "If that's a motion to adjourn, Bishop Neely, then I second the motion."

Hence the meeting was adjourned, thus saving Rev. Brooks from having to answer the question.

The preachers spilled out into the California night, some still grumbling. Rev. Flowers went down front to console Reggie, who was standing there alone looking dazed. The two of them just stood there for awhile, looking at each other without saying a word, like it hadn't dawned on them yet what had just happened. She had always been very fond of Reginald Brooks, going back to when as a boy he used to help her with Sunday school. He was very good with the younger children. Even then he was mature beyond his years.

"You know I'm not gay, don't you, Vi?" he finally said dolefully.

"Why didn't you just say that, Reggie, when Rev. Wright asked the question?" she replied, thinking that had he done that then all that animosity could have been avoided.

"Because I think we black people shouldn't be asking that question of each other. It divides us as a people. One's sexual orientation should be one's own business, and no one else's. We are all God's children, made in his image, and that includes gays," he said.

Before Rev. Flowers could reply with something apt from the Bible, someone walked up behind them and said, "I agree with you, Rev. Brooks. It's time we black people begin dealing with our homophobia." It was Rev. Bowman, the young female minister who sat next to Rev. Flowers during the meeting. Rev. Flowers thought she had left with the other preachers.

"Thanks for coming tonight, Evelyn," he said. The two of them hugged warmly.

Rev. Flowers' eyes got big. Was Reggie's friend a lesbian? she wondered, now renewing her doubts about Reggie. It was all so confusing, she thought.

****

Walking to her car after the meeting, Rev. Flowers regretted that the meeting had failed. "What makes it so sad is that Reggie didn't even get a chance to tell them about the fine work he's doing with the AIDS children," she said to herself as she remembered that just the other day Reggie told her that he was spending more and more of his time looking for couples who might be interested in adopting the sick children who had no parents or relatives.

"It isn't easy finding adoptive parents for these children. But when we do, it's so gratifying," he told her. "I took this white couple to the nursery at the hospital last week and showed them this three-month-old Mexican boy born addicted to heroin. The baby had been given up by his teenage mother. I told them that the tests showed that the little guy had the AIDS antibodies, and that he had a better than 50 percent chance of developing full-fledged AIDS. 'I don't care. We want him,' the wife said without hesitation, without even consulting with her husband who was also standing there at the child's crib. 'God has answered our prayers,' she said as she picked up the child and kissed his little brown face. She wanted to take him home then and there."

Rev. Flowers wished that Rev. Wright and the others tonight could have heard that tender story. If they had, they would have seen that Reggie was doing God's work.

Chapter Fourteen

Rev. Flowers' best friend was Bernice Jones, her longtime hairdresser. It was an odd friendship. When she moved to Los Angeles some years ago to establish her church, Viola needed a new hairdresser, so she asked around. A parishioner told her about this black hairdresser named Bernice, said to be not only very good but very cheap. That Bernice was inexpensive was a big selling point with Rev. Flowers, who was just starting out on her own and had to watch her spending. At the time Bernice was doing people's hair in her kitchen. The parishioner warned Rev. Flowers, however, that Bernice was very unreliable. Rev. Flowers tried her, liked the way she did her hair, and used her ever since, but it wasn't easy. Because she constantly struggled to pay her rent, Bernice moved around a lot without bothering to tell her customers. Thus it was hard to keep track of her.

In the early days of their relationship, several times Rev. Flowers literally had to track Bernice down to get her hair done. That Bernice's telephone stayed disconnected much of the time due to unpaid phone bills didn't help matters any. Unable to contact her on the telephone, Viola would go to Bernice's house or shop (if she had a shop) expecting to get her hair done, and find that Bernice was no longer there.

Usually the new occupant of the building had no idea where Bernice had moved to. "Maybe she just pulled up stakes and left town," one Korean merchant suggested, who had opened a nail salon where Bernice had once done black women's heads. Bernice was so whimsical in how she ran her business that it never occurred to her that she had an obligation to notify her customers, particularly her regulars like Rev. Flowers, when she moved her shop. But because Bernice was so good, and not wanting to get a new hairdresser, most of her customers, including Rev. Flowers, always made the effort to find her.

Like a private detective, Rev. Flowers hunted down and followed Bernice to ten different locations over the years. Once when Bernice was missing, someone told Viola Flowers that they believed Bernice had move to somewhere in the Crenshaw area. So Rev. Flowers went to that area and looked for her, checking door to door and looking through plate-glass windows. When Rev. Flowers was walking down the street looking desultorily into stores and shops, someone stuck her head out the door of a low-rent storefront across the street and yelled, "Vi!"

Rev. Flowers stopped and looked, and there was Bernice in the doorway, with a pair of scissors in her hand and a big grin on her face. "I wondered what happened to you," she told Rev. Flowers nonchalantly when the latter was snugly ensconced in the chair. Bernice always made it sound like it was Rev. Flowers who had disappeared without telling anybody. "That's Bernice," Rev. Flowers would laugh when discussing Bernice with others. She liked Bernice despite her flakiness that could drive you crazy at time. Notwithstanding that Bernice wasn't religious and never went to church and could curse like a Portuguese sailor, Vi considered the skinny, long-armed woman a good friend.

One day Bernice finally put down roots in a corner of Freddie's Barbershop where she and Freddie, a male, shared the rent. The barbershop/beauty parlor was located on Vermont Avenue in an area near downtown Los Angeles. They had two barber chairs a piece, although Bernice needed only one. They shared the toilet, wash basins and hairdryers in the backroom, an arrangement that benefited both of them. The men's side of the barbershop/beauty parlor was always loud with plenty of laughing, joking, and arguing about sports, especially about the Dodgers and the Lakers. Surprisingly, Freddie did a fairly good job of keeping cursing down, as well as keeping out the panhandlers, common drunks and dope dealers, even though a few of his customers would sometimes come in stoned or inebriated. Despite the sign on the wall advising that the pay phone was for customers only, many tenants from the dilapidated apartment building on the corner would come in and use the pay phone.

As good friends, Rev. Flowers and Bernice had few secrets between them. On some matters Viola talked only to God, on other matters only to Albert. But on many matters she needed to talk only to Bernice, and they talked by phone several times a week. Bernice, however, always called Viola, because Viola could never get through to the beauty shop. "Girl, it's easier to reach the President of the United States than it is to get through to you. Your phone stays busy. You should have the phone company take a look at your phone line. Maybe something's wrong with it," Vi told Bernice once after trying to reach her for two straight hours, getting only a busy signal. "I even tried praying, but that didn't work, either," Rev. Flowers joked. What she wanted to talk about wasn't particularly important. She just wanted to talk.

"There's nothing wrong with our phone. We just can't keep all those niggers off of it," Bernice answered good-naturedly. She realized her faux pas when Viola made a dill pickle face. Rev. Flowers didn't like it when Bernice used the word "nigger," not even in jest. Early in their relationship, Rev. Flowers gave her a long stern history lesson on that word.

Because the telephone at the beauty parlor stayed constantly busy, and because Bernice didn't trust the privacy of cell phones that were just coming into vogue, Vi tried to persuade Bernice to get a computer so they could communicate by e-mail. "Why not try it. It's easy to use," she told Bernice who frowned and said, "I don't want a computer. I don't want all them bugs crawling all over my house." "They're not talking about those kinds of bugs," Vi had to laugh because the term meant computer programming glitches, not insects.

Albert often kidded Viola about liking to hang out at the barbershop/beauty parlor with all those gamblers and thieves. (Albert didn't get his haircuts at Freddie's. He used a more upscale African American barbershop near Baldwin Hills.) Albert's gamblers and thieves allusion was because Viola had told him about all the goings-on at the barbershop.

For instance, she told him about a man named Willie who regularly came into the shop hawking clothes and jewelry. She told Albert that she feared the man was a shoplifter. "Buying from people like that is how many people in the ghetto get extra nice things," she told him, repeating what Bernice had told her. "I'm not condoning it, Vi. I'm only explaining the realities of the black community," Bernice had added.

"One day Willie came in selling diamond earrings at ridiculously low prices that he claimed were very valuable," Viola told Albert. "Bernice was about to buy a set until she saw the look on my face." Viola was referring to that "Shame on you!" look that, according to Bernice, she sometimes had when someone in the shop said or did something she thought crossed the moral line.

Albert laughed that big hearty laugh of his, "Knowing Bernice, she probably had him come back when you weren't there." He knew that a streetwise person like Bernice wouldn't deny herself a great bargain merely because it came from a thief or shoplifter.

"You might be right, but at least she respects me enough not to do it in my presence," Vi said proudly.

Oddly enough, Rev. Flowers respected Bernice in return. She liked the flaky hairdresser. Bernice was very different from most people. For instance, unlike most of Vi's friends, Bernice had no problem with the meaning of life. She just took life as it came. In the beauty shop around all those religious New Testament black folks, whenever religion came up Bernice would just roll her big eyes with annoyance, and change the conversation. Viola knew Bernice didn't believe in God.

"If it's possible that some humanlike thing created the world, then it's just as possible that some frog-like or snake-like thing did it. And I'm not ready to worship either a frog or a snake. I'll just wait until the scientists come up with something better," she laughed the first time she and Viola Flowers discussed religion. In Bernice's mind, Rev. Flowers' Bible proved nothing.

While most women who came to the shop believed in Jesus, there were a few who held the New Age view about God being Love and Love being God, and it was that force that created the world. To those women, Bernice would only say, “That's fine with me, if that’s what you wish to believe.” This was a remarkable point of view from a black female who had quit school in the tenth grade and whose knowledge of science came mostly from the Discovery Channel, her favorite TV viewing. Indeed, Bernice was one of the few black women Rev. Flowers knew who didn't attribute her strength and well-being to some spiritual power. “What I am all stems from my carbon-based existence,” Bernice would tell her religious customers in that matter-of-fact way of hers, and she would leave it at that. That view alarmed many of her Bible-quoting customers. But not Viola, who liked Bernice for the honest person that she was.

In fact Rev. Flowers secretly admired Bernice for her strong sense of independence. For her strong sense of knowing who she was, for good or bad. The two women were such opposites. Rev. Viola Flowers believed that the Christian Bible explained nearly everything. To her there was no doubt that God so loved the world that he gave his only begotten son, Jesus. For Bernice the Bible explained nothing, save a few rules about how to behave, most of which were now very outdated or rusty from nonuse.

On her part, Bernice liked Rev. Flower because for a church lady she was a very down-to-earth person. “Vi has an excellent sense of humor. She’s very comfortable around ordinary folks, and ordinary folks are comfortable around her,” she would say about Rev. Flowers. There was a great deal of truth in Bernice’s statement. For when in the beauty parlor Rev. Flowers was just one of the girls. No special favors or privileges. When in the shop she rarely rendered value judgments, and she always waited her turn like any other customer, usually bringing her own magazine. She never brought her Bible to read while waiting because she didn’t want to be conspicuous or make the other customers feel self-conscious. Whenever some customer who knew that Viola Flowers was a preacher would forget she was there and say something naughty or untoward, the customer would look embarrassed and apologize to Rev. Flowers, who would simply wave it off as being unimportant.

From their side of the shop, the men were always apologizing to her for something or another. By and large, the men had dirtier mouths and minds than the women. Rev. Flower would just smile that understanding smile of hers and turned back to reading or conversing with the female customers. Usually, however, she was so non-intrusive that the other customers in the beauty shop hardly noticed she was there. When leaving, she would turn and say to the male side of the shop before going out the door, "Good afternoon, gentlemen," and the room would become quiet and respectful. Almost without fail, those who didn't know her would feel compelled to ask who she was. "That's Rev. Flowers, the pastor of the Church of God & Spirit," Freddie would answer proudly. Sometimes a male customer would comment on her shapely legs, or her nice ass, or how attractive she was for a lady preacher.

Bernice liked working on Rev. Flowers' head because her hair was very easy to work with. It offered a hairdresser so many possibilities. "You have such big beautiful eyes, Vi. Let me give you a cut that'll do them justice," Bernice would advise Viola from time to time. Sometimes she would try to persuade Rev. Flowers to have a complete beauty makeover. "I think you could get away with a little more makeup if we did it right," she would say, cognizant of how conservative Rev. Flowers' congregation was. Then she would step back and examine Rev. Flowers' face like an artist would a painting.

"I wouldn't dare," Viola would laugh girlishly. Pondering those beauty possibilities always gave Rev. Flowers much pleasure, even if she never acted on them.

One day the man who ran a small clothing store two doors down stopped by the shop and showed the ladies some expensive woman's clothes he had just picked up cheap from a fire sale in the garment district, which included the most gorgeous dress imaginable that was Rev. Flowers' size. Of course Bernice insisted that Viola try it on. Laughing in that little girl fashion of hers, Rev. Flowers took the dress to the backroom and slip it on. All the women in the beauty parlor gathered around to see how she looked in it. She posed for them like a high fashion model, and everyone laughed at her silliness. They all thought she looked gorgeous in the dress, and urged her to buy it.

"Take it, Vi. You look great in it. It fits you to a T," Bernice urged strongly.

While she liked the dress because it showed off her nice figure to great avail, Rev. Flowers knew she could never wear anything that daring. Yet she smiled devilishly when she thought of what Albert would say if he saw her in it. He liked it when she used a little makeup every once in awhile or really dressed up on special occasions. When they first got married he used to buy her flimsy see-through things from Victoria's Secret which she made him return, even though secretly it flattered her. "Baby, what's wrong with wearing this just when you and me are having a quiet night at home together?" he said with disappointment before re-boxing the garment so it could be returned.

"Albert used to be so much fun in the old days," she thought, defining the old days as the time before he started running around with his new white born-again friends. Then in her mind's eye she saw herself posing for Manny Scott in that sexy dress. She saw Manny's big white smile, his bulging eyes, and his rising crotch. It didn't take much to get him sexually aroused, she couldn't help from remembering. The thought made her smile. "Viola Flowers, you're being a very bad girl. Behave yourself," she scolded herself mockingly.

Seeing the faraway mirth on Vi's face, Bernice asked her what was so funny.

"It's a lovely dress, Bernice. But my parishioners would run me out of town if I showed up at church in something this bold," she said, handing Bernice back the dress so she could give it back to the man waiting out front.

Truthfully Rev. Flowers regretted that she couldn't buy the garment.

Chapter Fifteen

The clock on the wall told Rev. Flowers that it was time for her to go the hospital to visit sick parishioners, but first she had to take the pies that she and her neighbor Maude baked that afternoon over to the church next door. She had a headache and really didn't feel like going out. She was bothered by something Maude had told her earlier while they were peeling peaches for the pies.

Maude revealed that her teenage daughter Megan was pregnant, and that they were considering getting an abortion. Rev. Flowers had known Megan since she was a baby. "Yesterday Megan told me that she has missed a couple of her periods. She thinks she's pregnant," Maude told her in confidence, "Vi, she's only sixteen. What should I do?"

Despite Viola Flowers' rather fundamentalist religious views, Maude valued her advice. From the day when her daughter told her last year that a couple of girls at her school had gotten pregnant, Maude feared the same might happen to Megan as well. She knew that her daughter was sexually active, for the two of them had talked about it. Maude regarded herself a liberal. She had taught her daughter how to say no and about safe sex. While she strongly believed in a woman's right to choose, Maude hadn't imagined how difficult that choice could be when the woman involved was your own sixteen-year-old daughter, and she had gotten bags under her eyes from worrying about Megan.

Rev. Viola Flowers sat in silence for a long while before answering Maude's question. Then she told Maude gravely, "Pray and ask God to help you make the right decision."

Her answer was short and sweet, and her advice surprised Maude who had expected a vastly different answer. In fact Maude was disappointed. She knew Rev. Flowers held pro-life views, because one morning a few years ago when the two of them were having coffee in Vi's kitchen, a news report came on TV about the assassination of an abortion doctor in Buffalo, New York.

"Now those rightwing crazies are resorting to outright murder. Those killers should be executed when caught," Maude said at the time, which was a very extreme reaction for her since she didn't believe in capital punishment. Viola gave her white friend a harsh reproving look, but said nothing, but Maude could see from Viola's stony face that she believed the abortion doctor had gotten what he deserved.

The two neighbors continued visiting that afternoon like nothing had happened, but from that moment on, each knew the other's strong views on abortion. And from that day on, for sake of their friendship and because they were neighbors, they avoided the prickly subject altogether.

Today, however, Maude felt the need to talk to Viola frankly about Megan. She wanted badly to hear Vi's anti-abortion views, for she wasn't as confident about her own pro-choice views now that her own daughter was involved. She had hoped that Vi's strong pro-life views would subject her own views to more scrutiny.

But unbeknownst to Maude, somewhere along the way since the Buffalo shooting, Rev. Viola Flowers had modified her anti-abortion views. Because of what happened to Maxine, she had even quit speaking out against abortions from the pulpit. The same was true for personal and family counseling. Now while neither advising against nor for abortions, in addition to advising prayer, she gave young women in trouble pamphlets on the free women's health clinics in their area, just in case the material would be needed later. In her Christian mind she justified this as giving out information for better family planning and prenatal care.

Truthfully, she didn't want them to make the mistake that Maxine made. As she had done with Maude, now when asked for advice about the propriety of having an abortion, she merely told her parishioners to pray and see what Jesus said about the matter, in effect telling them to trust their own conscience after conferring with God.

Disappointed by that vague answer, parishioners would invariably press Rev. Flowers for more specific moral guidance.

"But would getting an abortion be wrong in the eyes of the Lord?" they would ask her in their frustration. Unmoved Rev. Flowers would simply reply, "Ask the Lord that question, and trust what He tells you. It's a matter that concerns only you, Him, and your doctor. God loves you and only wants what's best for you." Then she would leave it at that.

Rev. Flowers' changed attitude baffled Maude. Most people, including Maude, were unaware that Rev. Flowers stopped opposing abortions after that awful day when she and Lettie had that big argument about Maxine.

****

Maude's family was one of several white families still living in Rev. Flowers' interracial Los Angeles neighborhood. Rev. Flower was the first African American to move into that neighborhood after her church bought the church and parsonage from a white church that moved to the San Fernando Valley. She and her family were then followed by a few other black families and some Mexican families. The Japanese Americans had lived in the neighborhood for decades. Rev. Flowers was very proud of how diverse her congregation was. She was particularly proud of her Mexican church members since there were so few non-Catholic Mexicans in Los Angeles.

Chapter Sixteen

Bishop Neely had sent for her, and Rev. Flowers had no idea what he wanted. She hadn't seen him since that night at Rev. Brooks' big meeting with the black ministers. She had heard the bad news that he had a stroke and she had sent him a get-well card.

"Please go right up, Rev. Flowers. The doctor has him confined to bed. It's the first bedroom on the left at the top of the stairs," Bishop Neely's wife told Rev. Flowers after giving her a warm greeting at the front door. Rev. Flowers didn't know Mrs. Neely very well. Unlike her famous husband who was always on television or whose picture stayed in the newspapers, Mrs. Neely was a very private person content to remain at home in that big rambling white house of theirs and care for their many grandchildren. She knew Mrs. Neely was a regular radio listener of hers because she had called in once and requested a prayer for an ailing loved one.

Rev. Flowers found Bishop Neely out of bed, in his pajamas, robe and slippers, sitting in a big rocking chair by the window. He was reading. She had brought her Bible because she knew that whatever their discussion would be, they would end up praying together before parting. He looked up and said. "Good afternoon, Rev. Flowers. Thanks for coming. Please excuse the robe and pajamas, but my doctor doesn't want me going downstairs for awhile."

He pointed to the armchair across from him. "Have a seat." He put his book down. She glanced at the title: *Christianity: Scourge or Blessing to the Human Race?* She knew he was an eminent theologian with high offices in many national religious organizations.

"The Lord must've thought I was getting too big for my britches and knocked me down a peg or two," he jested, speaking of his stroke. Save a little slurring in his speech that was hardly noticeable, his condition wasn't as bad as she had expected to find. She was pleased he was recovering so well.

She liked Bishop Neely. Although a Methodist he was how she mentally pictured her grandfather who died before she was born: a strong, proud black man who was a leader not only of other men, but of other leaders. A man of great faith. Of great conscience. “Even the Pope in Rome would humbly bow and kiss his ring,” was the joke about Bishop Neely among black ministers. One could see Bishop Neely's specialness in the very way he walked and carried himself, and in his grand manners and speech. Even white people felt compelled to address him as " Sir" when dealing with him.

She appreciated greatly that Bishop Neely always took her seriously, both as a person and a preacher. He never regarded her lightly as many other male ministers had done. And she was very grateful for that. Because of her color, her sex, and her denomination, all her professional life she had to fight to be taken seriously by her male colleagues, especially her black male colleagues.

Surprisingly, being black was the least of her burdens as a black female gospel minister. Being a female minister was a much tougher proposition for her. It always amazed her how easy it was for prejudiced male theologians to find biblical justifications to exclude women from leadership roles in the church. She had learned at an early age that back in biblical days men were very prejudice against women, and that this prejudice was reflected in the holy writings of the time.

When she first began studying the Bible her father taught her that there was much in the Bible that couldn't be taken literally. “It depends on how you interpret it,” he told her whenever she came to him as a child with questions about something troubling or conflicting in the Bible, “Your faith in Jesus will guide you through all the fiction and falsity that's in the Bible. When reading the Bible you must make allowances for yesterday's biases, particularly yesterday's male biases,” he told her.

When in Bible college a professor of hers told her class once that both the Old and New Testaments were nothing but a collection of stories that the Abrahamic faiths had made holy, some made-up, some true, told largely by men for men, often to the detriment of women.

"The Bible contains many biases and misconceptions that no longer exist. Witness how our religious views on child-rearing and adultery have changed over the centuries. In primitive Israel, for example, obeying the rules of society was very important. Disobeying those rules was considered such an evil that parents of a rebellious child, for instance, were required to take that child outside the village and allow the entire community to stone the child to death."

Then he told the class, "We wouldn't tolerate people treating children like that today. Our thinking has changed. Yet that edict still remains in the Bible." (This professor was booted out of her college before the year was over because of his "liberal" teachings.)

Because so many people were lumping all Christians together and tarnishing them with one brush, Rev. Flowers found that being a saved Christian, or a born-again Christian as the white folks would say, was becoming more difficult every day. Moreover, because so many people were dismissing them all as "rightwing nuts" or "religious fanatics," she was finding it increasingly harder to get respect as a gospel minister in many mainstream circles. She felt this was very unfair, for she was neither rightwing nor fanatical. While she didn't believe in abortions and was saddened that so many of them were being performed around the world, she no longer believed in blocking other people from getting them.

There were other religious snobberies that she sometimes had to put up with because of her gospel faith. Many white people mockingly called members of her church "holy rollers" because of their rollicking religious services. Some in the black community saw her particular faith as being at the bottom of the religion totem pole, just a notch above storefront Pentecostal churches.

When a little girl Viola Flowers sometimes felt that her Baptist and Methodist playmates looked down on her because she attended a holiness church that believed in the holy ghost and where the congregants shouted "hallelujah" aloud and danced in church to tambourines and swinging pianos. In those days many children in her church were ashamed to admit at school what church they belonged to. But not her. She always walked with her head high among her snickering friends.

"People laughed at Jesus, too, Viola. So ignore them. Among all of Jesus' children, you're walking the closest to God," her father told her when she told him about the razzing she sometimes took at school due to her religion. Ergo she was proud of her church. She was proud of its history, and appreciated her church's struggles over the years to arrive at a consistent body of religious beliefs that would allow them to worship God in the right way—their way. She was proud that both her grandfather and father had played important roles in those struggles.

Even today because her church was a small gospel church of ordinary working people, some black ministers in town with larger and more prestigious congregations saw her as being beneath them. Not Bishop Neely, however. He regarded her as a peer. As an equal. They had worked well together on many citywide committees. On one committee she served as his co-chairperson.

"You're probably wondering why I sent for you," Bishop Neely said.

"Your message sounded urgent," Rev. Flowers answered respectfully.

"I tried to reach Rev. Brooks, but he's out of town. I wanted to let you and Rev. Brooks know that I'm with you in your efforts to galvanize the black ministry in the fight against AIDS. You two are going to need all the help you can get. It's going to be difficult getting some of our black brethren to face this thorny problem."

Dumbfounded, she looked at Bishop Neely and wondered where he had gotten the preposterous idea that she was one of the organizers of Rev. Brooks' group. She wasn't one of the organizers or even a member. Except for helping Reggie get the word out about his big meeting, she had nothing to do with the group. She had just as many doubts about the venture as the other preachers at the meeting that night. While it was true that she and Reggie Brooks were good friends, she too found homosexuality disturbing, and she didn't want to be a part of any effort that condoned it.

She started to tell Bishop Neely this, but he, believing she was one of his group, continued outlining the difficulties that lay ahead of them.

"Too many of us black preachers foolishly believe that AIDS is a gay disease caused by the wrath of God." Then he chuckled lightly, "Personally I think God has more important things to do than punishing people for loving each other."

"What about Leviticus 18:22, Bishop Neely? Or Romans 1:26 to 27," Rev. Flowers felt forced to say, her eyes bulging. How could Bishop Neely talk like that in light of those scriptures in the Bible? she wondered, now more perplexed than ever.

Her discussions with Rev. Brooks had never reached the point where she felt the need to invoke the Bible. For the most part she and Rev. Brooks restricted their discussion of AIDS to the sick children. Since their clash that day on their way to Children's Hospital, they had carefully avoided the controversial subject of homosexuality.

Therefore, there was never a need for her and Reggie to discuss the *Book of Leviticus* where the Lord said that men lying down with men as though they were man and woman was an abomination. Going even farther, *Leviticus* 20:13 said those men should be put to death.

She realized that few, if any, clergymen today, including most fundamentalist Christians, would interpret those passages as actually calling for the physical death of homosexuals. Some of her minister friends read them to mean that homosexuals should be cast out to the Devil, while other clergymen she knew believed those passages in *Leviticus* calling for death should be totally ignored as outdated.

She came down somewhere in the middle in her thinking on the matter. She belonged to that group of ministers who didn't believe the Bible actually called for killing homosexuals, but instead called for warning them about their abominable behavior, with AIDS being God's concrete example of what can happen if this behavior wasn't stopped. This interpretation also included praying for them.

Bishop Neely stilled his rocking chair and leaned forward. "What about Leviticus 18:22?" he said crustily. Her question surprised him.

She explained nervously her understanding of that bit of the Scripture.

He replied in that professorial way of his, "In Romans 1:26 and 27, Paul doesn't condemn homosexuality. He merely tries to explains it, albeit not very clearly. For Paul homosexuality was what could happen to people who practice idolatry. Worshipping and serving false gods and images were very serious offenses in those days. That was what Paul was worried about. Those were the practices that God abhorred, not homosexuality. Paul was only speaking of homosexuality as God's punishment for idolaters. Back then idolatry was seen as a far worst thing than homosexuality. Whether you agree or disagree with Paul's understanding of the gospel, the passage of time has made much of this moot. People's thinking has changed over time. Nowadays we're simply not that concerned about idolatry. Most of those passages are now outdated."

His handsome old face became hard as he frowned and said, "This wouldn't be the first time that Paul's been unclear about the gospel. He was also very muddled on the race question. It's clear in Galatians 3:28 that Paul understood that God condemned distinctions based on race and class. Had he taken the time to draw out the social ramifications of his understanding of what it meant to be 'all one in Christ' as set forth in Galatians 3:28, we might have avoided all the class and racial conflicts over the centuries."

He then added, "Had Paul made the topic of manumission an explicit directive of the gospel, and not danced around it as he did, slavery might have been nipped in the bud. I believe with other religious scholars that Paul should've told his friend Philemon that slavery was inconsistent with the gospel, and that as a Christian he, Philemon, had a duty to free Onesimus and his other slaves. Can you imagine what western civilization would look like today had Paul stepped up to the plate and clearly explained what he meant when he said: 'Ye are all one in Christ Jesus.' Had he done his job properly, perhaps we African Americans would have escaped slavery."

Bishop Neely yawned; Rev. Flowers could see he was getting a little tired.

"Please forgive me for getting off the subject, Rev. Flowers," he said, "I'm an old man and I wander occasionally. I wanted to discuss HIV and AIDS, not homosexuality. I just wanted to thank you and Rev. Brook for getting things started. There's no greater cause in the black community today than stopping the spread of AIDS. And we ministers must lead the way."

While he talked, Rev. Flowers sat there feeling like a palmed bird, feeling trapped in events not of her making. The situation reminded her of that summer day when as a child she was downtown shopping with her mother. The two of them were about to go into F.W. Woolworth Dime Store when they heard the music of a marching band. When they looked down the street, a high-stepping circus parade turned the corner and moved their way.

"May I stay out here and watch, Mommy!" little Viola said excitedly, clapping her hands in glee at the approaching drums and trombones.

"You may stay out here and watch from the curb while I run into the store and pick up a few things. But stay put. Don't move. I'll be right back," her mother said before dashing into the store.

Little Viola watched from the curb in front of the store and didn't move from that spot as her mother had told her. It was a good place to view the parade. Then as the marching band approached, the crowd got larger and larger. Next the clowns came down the street making everyone laugh with their funny juggling and tumbling antics. The onlookers pointed and hollered, amused by the buffoonery. Having a good time, the crowd began moving down the street trying to keep up with the clowns, sweeping little

Viola along in the flow. Before she realized it, she was all the way down the street, nearly a whole block from the spot that her mother had warned her not to leave.

As she rushed back to Woolworth's, she saw her frightened mother looking every-which-way trying to find her.

"Here I am, Mommy!" she called to her mother, all the while trying to watch the elephants that were now passing by.

Her mother took little Viola by her shoulders and shook her furiously. "Didn't I tell you not to move from in front of the store! I trusted you! I let you stay outside by yourself to watch the parade! And I come out and find you a block away!" her mother scolded her severely. Her mother was angry not because she feared some harm might have befallen her daughter. She was furious because Viola had disobeyed her, something very uncharacteristic of her.

"But Mommy, I didn't move. Honest. I was just standing here minding my own business, and then all of a sudden I was way down there," the girl tried to explain, about to cry.

Rev. Viola Flowers felt the same way now. She hadn't joined Rev. Brooks' group. She hadn't moved. She was just minding her own business, and then all of a sudden she found herself being one of Rev. Brooks' top lieutenants.

But before she could explain, Bishop Neely spoke up, "When I'm back on my feet, you can count me in. Your radio program will be invaluable to us."

She said nothing. She was afraid to. Also she could see that he needed his nap now.

Before leaving they got down on their knees and prayed together.

Chapter Seventeen

In his white shirt starched and fresh from the cleaners, Albert Flowers struggled in the mirror with his tie. Tying bow ties always gave him trouble. He started wearing bow ties when he worked for the county and was elected an officer in his union. He thought bow ties made him looked like a real professional man. Now he wore them only on very special occasions. Viola hadn't seen him in a bow tie since the two of them attended a radio-awards ceremony a few years ago when she won the "Gospel Broadcaster of the Year Award." Seeing him having trouble with his tie, she walked over and fixed it for him. He looked very nice all dressed up like that. She saw why she became attracted to him after she had just broken up with Rev. Scott. "Life doesn't have to be perfect to be wonderful," she told herself when she and Albert started dating.

"I don't understand why we must get all dressed up like this just to go to a friend's house for dinner. I don't care if it is in Malibu," Viola fussed as she checked her stockings to see if her seams were straight. Albert had succeeded in getting her to wear a little makeup, something she seldom did. She even had on high heels.

"Mr. Burnum isn't my friend, exactly. He's a rich friend of Bob's who interested in making a big donation to my campaign," Albert said.

Even though she stood behind him, she still believed his running for Congress was a bad idea. "Why do you want to run for Congress when you already have your hands full? Why don't you guys get your shuttle business going smoothly first before taking on something else," she told Albert when he first informed her of his decision to run. "Also, what happened to that McDonald's franchise you guys were working on?" she added sarcastically. She was irked that in addition to all the other things Albert and Bob Haines were trying to do, now all of a sudden they were dabbling in politics.

Another reason she was irked was that she disliked the Republican Party, at least that branch of the party that Albert's crowd belonged to. While they said the right things, such as allowing prayer in public schools, supporting family values, and respecting the unborn, she didn't trust them. She thought they were hypocrites. They seemed driven by only one thing: their love of money and their love of the freedom to make even more of it. Now Albert was beginning to sound and behave like them. One day he said to her, "I was downtown this morning, Vi, and you can't walk ten feet without some filthy bum stopping you and asking for a handout. I gave them nothing. I told them I'd help them if they wanted to find work. But they didn't want jobs. They just wanted a few dollars to get drunk on."

Albert didn't used to talk like that. Before he became a businessman and when he worked for the union, he helped set up a program where county workers with drinking and drug problems could get help. "If the union doesn't help them, they'll be fired and maybe forced to live on the street. And God knows we don't need any more homeless. We have too many now," he said back in the good old days. In those days he didn't see the homeless as dirty bums who didn't deserve to live. He saw them as human beings who needed help. A few years ago when she briefly opened up the church to the homeless at night, Albert supported her 100 percent. She blamed his new Republican friends for the radical change in his thinking about the poor. It was a shame, she thought, because Albert used to be such a kind and generous person.

Albert checked the inside coat pocket of his blue serge suit to make sure he had enough good cigars with him. They were the cigars that another good white buddy of his had gotten from Cuba via Canada, which caused some controversy in their circle of conservative friends. Part of their group, especially the Cuban exiles, opposed buying the cigars because it helped Fidel Castro stay in power, a man they hatred almost as much as they hated President Bill Clinton. On the cigar issue Albert belonged to that other group of Republicans who preferred thinking of the cigars as being Canadian products, not Cuban, even though they took great delight in pointing out the cigars' Cuban origin when handing them out to people.

"Please remember, Vi, no talk about religion tonight, " Albert said to her one more time before they left the house. Unlike Albert's other white friends, Mr. Burnum wasn't a born-again Christian.

"I'll be good. I promise," Viola said, crossing her heart mockingly as they departed for the Malibu Colony a short ways up the coast from Los Angeles.

With Albert getting deeper into Republican politics every day, Viola found it increasingly difficult to stand by in silence. She found herself more and more at odds with his new circle of white friends. Sometimes it was embarrassing for Albert. But she felt she had an obligation to speak up because people like Rev. Falwell and Rev. Pat Robertson were giving evangelicalism a bad name.

"I don't see why it's necessary to be against welfare mothers just because you oppose abortions. Aren't we forgetting that Jesus' main concern was the welfare of the weak and poor, not the rich and the powerful," Rev. Flowers would argue with Albert's conservative friends. She would tell them that her faith in Jesus Christ was expansive enough to allow her to believe in family values and the Golden Rule without giving up her right to be critical of the rich and the mighty. When Albert's new friends complained about liberal judges, she would reply, "No, I don't think the courts have gone too far in protecting the rights of criminal defendants and the environment. I think the courts have the balance just about right."

When discussing crime with them, she would say, "I believe, as I'm certain that Jesus believed, that the best way to fight crime is to deal with the root causes of crime, such as unemployment and poor housing. Our youth must be given something positive to do to keep them out of trouble." Those frank opinions of hers often embarrassed Albert, so tonight he begged her to be discreet about her views. "I don't want to blow this, Vi. This is too important," he told her.

Bob Haines' rich friend lived in a wealthy gated beachside community of multimillion dollar homes famous because many film and rock stars lived there. The Burnum home was a large estate that sat on a cliff overlooking the ocean. The ever-present pounding of waves could be heard in the living room.

Bob Haines and his wife Alice were already there when Viola and Albert arrived. Bob was in the billiard room with Frank Burnum and a couple of men neither Violet nor Albert knew. Bob's wife Alice, along with the other Republican wives, was being escorted on a tour of the house by Mrs. Burnum, who had already showed them the guesthouse, the servants' quarters, the pool, and the cabaña.

Mrs. Burnum, who seemed like a friendly sort, saw Viola from outside and waved for her to join them. Although she wanted to stay with the men, Rev. Flowers reluctantly went out and joined the other wives.

Later as they walked to the dining room for dinner, Mr. Barnum asked Rev. Flowers softly, "What do you think of Al's running for Congress?" He gave her an inquisitive look.

"It's a Democratic district, and I don't know if the people there are ready for a Republican Congressman," she answered frankly.

"Are *you* ready for a Republican Congressman?" he said with razor sharpness as he observed her carefully through narrowed green eyes. He hadn't expected such a frank reply from her. This frankness both bothered and impressed him.

"What do I know. I'm just a minister of a small gospel church. I leave politics to the politicians," she said, backing off without really answering his question, feigning a smile, while regretting she had been so outspoken. She knew how important the dinner was to Albert. Before leaving home she promised him she would be very circumspect about what she said tonight.

She realized that since becoming a Republican Albert stayed on pins and needles about what she might say when the two of them were out socially with his white conservative friends. "You're so doggone honest and outspoken," Albert would tell her when they were alone.

In arranging their guests at the dinner table, the Burnums had split her and Albert up. They seated her on one side of the table and Albert on the other side. Frank Burnum sat at the head of the table between the two of them. Bob and Alice Haines had been unimportantly placed at the far end of the table. Knowing how cunning Albert's business friends were, Rev. Flowers doubted if the seating arrangement was by happenstance. When they arrived tonight she got the distinct impression that Frank Burnum and Bob Haines had already had their little talk. Clearly Albert was the one being checked out now, which made her all the more defensive.

Frank Burnum had been in many business partnerships prior to becoming very rich in auto parts with a national chain he had rescued from bankruptcy. He knew from bitter experience that a wife can make or break an enterprise. He had learned that often the man signing the contract with him wasn't his real partner, but the man's wife was. "I've kicked out more business partners and fired more company executives for being mere pawns of their wives than I care to remember," he would tell people, leaving no doubt that he was the kind of man who had to deal with the real power on the throne, not some flunky. And there was something about Rev. Flowers that told him that she might be the real power in the Flowers household, and that troubled him.

At dinner the conversation was mostly about First Lady Hilary Clinton, much to the amusement of everybody but Rev. Flowers, who didn't find what was being said funny at all. She was a Bill Clinton supporter. During dinner she could feel Mr. Burnum watching her warily. In fact all night long he eyed her like a tailor sizing up someone for a fitting.

After dinner Frank Burnum took the Flowers into his study so he could talk to them in private. Albert handed him a big fat cigar from his inside coat pocket before Burnum could offer him one from the humidor on his desk. It was a fast-draw contest that Albert won. Burnum put his glass of brandy down and sniffed the cigar as one would a rose and satisfaction glittered in his green eyes. "This is a very fine cigar, Al. Is it Cuban?" he asked.

"It's from Canada," Albert replied carefully since he didn't know where Mr. Burnum stood on the Cuban cigar question.

"Do you mind, Reverend?" Burnum turned and politely asked her permission before lighting up.

"Please, go right ahead," she said, trying not to show that she disapproved of smoking.

Before leaving home Albert had pointed out to her for the umpteenth time how important that dinner was. "Bob says that not only might Frank help finance my Congressional campaign, but he might even join us in that shopping center development we're working on," Albert told her. "He's been known to provide a little venture capital from time to time." Upon hearing about the shopping center, Rev. Flowers blinked, for she hadn't heard that idea before. What was she going to do with those two juveniles? she thought, meaning Albert and Bob Haines.

Behind the closed doors of his study Burnum turned to her and said, "Al should be in Washington, Rev. Flowers. We need more good people in Congress. I believe that to have less government, we need more good people in government." With arms folded, puffing his big cigar, he strutted back and forth in front of the French doors overlooking the ocean. "Man is most virtuous, most productive, and most beneficial to society when he's helping himself, not when he's being helped by government. It's this belief that makes us Republicans. Al shares this philosophy, which is why we want him in Congress. He's honest, industrious, hardworking, and cares about people," he said, then looked at Albert like he wanted to go over and put his arm around him fondly.

"He's for gun control. Did you know that, Mr. Burnum?" Rev. Flowers interposed bluntly. She just couldn't help herself. His arrogance had angered her. She figured that before this cocky white man said anything more about her Albert's running for Congress as a Republican, there was something he needed to know about her husband. "Not only is Albert for gun control, he's passionate about it. His nine-year-old niece was killed a few years ago in a drive-by shooting. If left to Albert he would get every single gun off the streets immediately. Even Mr. Haines, an avid gun collector, can't dissuade him on this point," she said proudly.

"No, I didn't know that." Burnum's eyes bulged from this bit of new information. He scratched his chin in thought and said, "I guess in that district being for gun control shouldn't hurt that much."

Then he looked at Albert and smiled, "Actually that might even help you. I doubt if there are many gun nuts living in that district anyway."

Then he asked good-naturedly, "You wouldn't happen to be pro-choice, would you, Al?"

"No, I'm violently opposed to abortions. They're against my religion," Albert answered quickly to make up for his gun control flaw. He glanced sheepishly over at Viola since he wasn't really that opposed to abortions. Like her, he only wished there wouldn't be so many of them.

"It doesn't matter," Mr. Burnum said with a hint of disappointment, "I only asked because I'm pro-choice, but that's another story, for another time." He turned back to Viola and said gravely, "The only thing that matters, Rev. Flowers, is that with the changed demographics, Al will make a good Republican candidate for that district." He puffed on his big cigar, and from the determined look on his face, it was clear the Republican Party had circled their Congressional District as important to their strategy to win back the U.S. Congress.

He faced Albert again. "You can win that seat, Al, and I'm willing to back you"

The three of them then discussed the campaign. Mr. Burnum let Albert do most of the talking. Relighting his cigar that had gone out, Albert said, "Bob and I see our campaign as a wagon with four wheels that will move us smoothly to victory in the primary. The four wheels are 1) smaller government, 2) lower taxes, 3) the right to life, and 4) school vouchers. We will stick to this message and not let ourselves be pushed to the left by other issues. In other words, we will stay in the wagon and satisfy our base. Bob thinks that staying in the wagon will also help me distinguish myself from my liberal Democratic opponent in the general election."

Thinking how much Albert now sounded like Bob Haines, Viola smiled to herself. She had heard Albert make that same little speech the other night in her kitchen when he was practicing it with Bob Haines. What Albert meant was that in the 1992 presidential campaign, Bill Clinton's campaign advisors came up with the clever slogan: "It's the economy, stupid," which was designed to keep the campaign focused and on message.

Bob Haines wanted something similar to help keep Albert's campaign focused and on message. Thus Albert and Bob Haines came up with the slogan: "Stay in the wagon." Originally the slogan was "stay in the wagon, stupid," but they changed it because Albert felt the "stupid" part could be construed as referring to him.

Initially Bob Haines wanted anti-gun control to be the fourth wheel on the wagon, but Albert refused to take such a position in his campaign. And on the issue of stricter immigration, Albert feared getting too close to Prop 187. The Republicans were still pissed off about the court ruling that declared the anti-immigration ballot measure unconstitutional. Even worse, Prop 187 had caused the Latino community to go bonkers, which resulted in huge Latino protests and voter registration drives. Thus not wanting to touch that issue, Albert and Bob Haines agreed on school vouchers as the fourth wheel of their campaign.

****

After dinner that night when the Flowers and the other guests headed for their cars, one of the wives said with disappointment about the Burnum household, "I didn't see a single Bible in that whole big house."

"He's probably a Jew," another wife offered a guess.

Rev. Flowers looked up and saw Frank Burnum, still puffing on Albert's cigar, standing on his balcony looking down at them. He looked very pleased.

Chapter Eighteen

Rev. Flowers felt like she was walking on air. She felt great because today she realized why she became a minister. Today she had seen the wonders of her work. Today everything made sense to her. She kicked off her shoes and sat down at her desk, very pleased with herself. At the risk of being immodest, she felt she deserved a big pat on the back. "Thank you, Jesus," she said, her hands folded as she looked skyward gratefully.

She had just returned from visiting her little sick friend in Children's Hospital. While sitting at the child's bedside it became clear to her that the child's regular AIDS treatment wasn't working. On each visit instead of finding improvement she found the little girl getting worse, so she decided to see if "laying on hands" would help. "What harm could be done?" she asked herself hopefully. "Please, Lord, guide me through this," she prayed silently as she took both of the little girl's hands and began praying. After awhile she experienced something that felt like electricity passing between them. It seemed to have worked, because the little girl stopped whimpering from her pain and fell peaceably off to sleep. When Rev. Flowers got up from her chair at the child's bedside, she was physically and emotionally spent. It was like all her energy had been passed into the body of the little girl.

"This has been a terrific day," she said with a big satisfied smile as she sat there in her office. She had never "laid on hands" before.

That night in her church service she did another thing that she had never done before in all her years of preaching. On impulse she "laid hands" on a crippled young man in a wheelchair who had been shot and paralyzed in a gang shooting. He had now found Jesus. Holding both of his hands as she did with the little girl in a hospital, Rev. Flowers prayed for him, and then commanded him to stand up on his feet.

She told him not to fear, for God was with him. With great effort he tried to obey her command and stood for a split second before plopping back down in his wheelchair in pain. It seemed to have worked a little, she thought. She wiped his brow and prayed for him again, all the while rubbing his hands gently. "I believe we made a little progress. That'll be enough for tonight," she told him before hugging him and returning to the pulpit. The congregation was amazed.

At home that night she realized that her laying of hands on the young man in the wheelchair hadn't been impulsive. Far from it. She was unconsciously practicing her healing powers. She wanted to strengthen those powers so she could help the little AIDS girl. She hoped Jesus had passed some of his healing power on to her as he did to his disciples in Luke 9, verse 12. She personally knew many evangelists who had this heavenly gift. And they were not charlatans doing amusing tricks in circus tents, but real ministers doing good healing work as a part of their regular church ministries. Her friend Rev. Otis James, for instance, healed sick people on national television. She also knew this white woman minister in Riverside County who drew people to her church from as far away as Los Angeles because of her healing gifts.

Many of the older members of the church who knew him said her father had healing powers. Aunt Belle told her once that when a boy her father couldn't walk past a stray sick cat or an injured bird without wanting to take it home and nurse it. "Your father really wanted to be a veterinarian, not a preacher. When small he used to heal the sick animals in our neighborhood. We were living in Missouri at the time. In those days in certain outlying sections of the city, people still kept livestock in their back yards, even milk cows.

'Call the pastor's son. He's got a knack for healing animals,' church parishioners and neighbors would say when one of their animals became ill," Aunt Belle said. Viola knew that her father pooh-poohed the notion that he had divine powers. He would say with modesty, "I have no special healing powers. Sometimes I'm just lucky and can figure out what's wrong with an animal and can help it a little. Animals have ways of telling you when they're not feeling well. If you listen closely, sometimes you can understand what they're saying."

This unbelieving attitude of her father that he had no special healing powers always angered her grandfather tremendously, Aunt Belle told her, saying that Viola's grandfather would accuse his son, Viola's father, of looking a gift horse in the mouth. "You sometimes understand what the animals are saying? Is that what you just said, boy?"

Bishop Crombie would scold his young son Tom Jr. brutally, "Nonsense! That was God working his will on that animal through you. So give God credit. When you help people with their critters, tell them it was the Lord, not you, who did the healing." He would sometimes give Tom Jr. a hard slap on the head, Aunt Belle said. According to her, Tom Sr., her brother, was very quick with his hands when it came to disciplining Tom Jr. "Your healing powers would be even stronger if you got down on your knees once in awhile and blessed Jesus for giving you this gift," Tom Sr. would tell Tom Jr. There would always be a little envy in his voice. "What gift, Poppa? I don't have special powers," Tom Jr. would try to explain.

It wasn't that Tom Jr. didn't appreciate the Lord's role in what he did with animals. He did. He knew God was the guiding force in everything he did, and everything that happened or will happen. He simply believed it was more a matter of information about the animal than some divine intervention. He didn't think that God, after giving him a brain, needed to stand around all day telling him how to use it. To Tom Jr., that would be a waste of the Lord's precious time.

Tom Jr. loved animals and wanted to go to veterinarian school, but his father opposed the idea and insisted that he go to the seminary as they had originally planned. "You don't need a school to help you heal animals. The Lord has already given you that ability. You just need to pray more," his father would tell him. Tom Sr. loved his only son dearly, but he wanted him to stick to the teachings in the Bible, rather than always looking for answers outside in the world. He also wanted him to concentrate more on church affairs. "I need your help here in the church, Tom. I'm planning on you to help me run the national church someday," he constantly told his son.

Rev. Flowers agreed with her grandfather that her father lacked the proper appreciation of the wondrous gift that God had given him. Aunt Belle also had that gift, which might explain why she became a nurse. Now Rev. Flower was convinced that she had that gift as well. She remembered when only six years old overhearing her parents discussing whether she was old enough to be "saved." Viola's mother felt at the time that Viola was too young for that awesome spiritual responsibility. Her father disagreed. "Viola's old enough, honey. She's one of God's miracles. She was born understanding his words."

Rev. Flowers recalled those words like they were spoken just yesterday. "If I'm one of God's miracles, then maybe God has given me special healing powers," she speculated to herself. For the sake of little Elizabeth in the hospital, she certainly hoped so.

One night she got down on her knees and spoke to God about it. "I once promised you that I'd always be honest with you, O Lord. That I'd always tell you what's on my mind. So I'm telling you now. Please increase my healing powers. Please help me heal that little girl. I've never asked you for much, but now with all my heart and soul I'm begging you for this. Please, God, please," she pleaded.

Chapter Nineteen

Rev. Mike had just left. It had been awhile since he last dropped by the church. When Beulah arrived for work at five that morning he was asleep in his old jalopy in the church's parking lot. Months ago he promised Rev. Flowers and Beulah that he would build additional shelving in the pantry. After taking measurements, he took the money needed for the lumber, told Beulah that he would be back in an hour, and got into his old car and headed for the lumber yard a few blocks away. That was nearly four months ago. Now there he was, curled up in the front seat of his car sound asleep, his back seat loaded down with lumber.

When Beulah's coffee aromas woke him up, he came into the kitchen of the church and said good morning. Without saying another word, he went into the toilet, took a leak, washed his face and hands, and came out and helped himself to a cup of coffee and a doughnut. Still without saying anything, he went out to his car and brought in the lumber and his tools, and resumed building the shelves in the pantry. No explanation. No excuses. Nothing. He just went back to work with the aplomb of someone just returning from lunch. Aware of Rev. Mike's eccentricities, Beulah only chuckled and began fixing him breakfast as she usually did when he dropped by in the mornings.

When he finished building the shelves, he went to the church office and notified Rev. Flowers that he was done. He likewise gave her no whys or wherefores of his four-month disappearance. Like Beulah, she too just took him in stride. She went with him to inspect his carpentry work. "This is a beautiful job you've done, Rev. Mike. I'm pleased you were able to get us all this additional space. We really need it for all the donated canned goods we have stacked up in the hallway," she told him when the two of them returned to her office so she could pay him.

"How much do I owe you?" she asked, reaching into her desk drawer for the petty cash box. As he usually did, he shrugged noncommittally and left it up to her to decide what he should be paid. Sometimes he refused to accept any pay for things he did and considered his breakfast or lunch as sufficient payment, and at other times he gladly took the money. Beulah believed his policy depended on whether or not he needed money for gas or car repairs.

Today he quickly took the few dollars that Rev. Flowers offered him. Next they discussed the church garden, with him telling Rev. Flowers that when crossing the garden to the kitchen he noticed a few dead branches on some of her peach trees that needed pruning. He said that if she wished, he would prune them the next time he stopped by. She accepted his offer and thanked him in advance. He apologized for not being able to stay longer and left.

Rev. Flowers always enjoyed it whenever Rev. Mike stopped by and spent a few minutes with her. She enjoyed those spiritual moments. He reminded her of a traveling monk: the way he would just drop into her office, take a seat, close his eyes, and blend into the silence of the morning. She couldn't explain it, but like with the songbirds in the trees outside her office window, his shabby presence was always comforting. Sometimes he would ask her to pray with him. He never talked much.

He was particularly reticent about his own ministry. She felt this was a shame, inasmuch as there was much she wanted to talk to him about that could be beneficial to both their ministries, especially on how they could work together. Often her church had more donated canned goods and other food stuff than they needed for their programs, which they then had to give away to other charities.

What's more, quite often Beulah had lots of cooked food left over at the end of the day that she would gladly save for Rev. Mike if she could depend on him to stop by and pick it up from their cooler. She knew Rev. Mike could use the food, because people had seen him distributing food to the homeless at various places downtown. However, because they never knew when he would show up, Beulah usually threw the leftover food into the garbage. This was such a pity with all the hunger in the city.

Rev. Mike's reluctance to talk about himself or his ministry was very puzzling to Rev. Flowers. Unlike Beulah, she didn't think he was retarded; she had seen him around at the hospitals and jails visiting the sick and incarcerated. She once ran into him at a city council meeting that was taking up homeless issues, where he got up and spoke and made many good points. Whenever she tried to raise the topic of his ministry with him, he would always change the subject, which was so baffling. Was he ashamed of his outdoor ministry? Maybe he wasn't a real minister at all. Maybe he was just a slightly touched-in-the-head homeless bum as Beulah maintained. He was such an odd duck.

Yet there was something about Rev. Mike that made her respect him. Perhaps it was the kindness in his eyes. Maybe it was the hallowed way he carried himself. Maybe it was how he could always be counted upon to get something done in that unreliable way of his. Or maybe it was the compassionate nature of his prayers, prayers that always sought help and solace for others, and never himself. Prayers that always went to the essence of the matter. She knew he wasn't a stupid man, for his prayers were not the prayers of a fool. In many ways he reminded her of Jesus.

There were many rumors in the community about who Rev. Mike really was and where he came from. One rumor was that he was a defrocked priest who was booted out of his church in the Haight-Ashbury District in San Francisco in the 1960s for holding sex workshops in the church basement that featured lectures on free love, masturbation, and oral sex.

It was said that for field trips he sent his parishioners out to porno movies, girlie bars and strip joints which San Francisco was so famous for at the time. In those days San Francisco was the land of the free spirits where every night young people, when not protesting the horrors of the Viet Nam War, filled the streets with flowers in their hair, hugging, dancing, tripping and proclaiming free love. According to the rumor, Rev. Mike, then Father Mike a Catholic priest, became brain-damaged on acid.

Rev. Flowers didn't believe that rumor.

Another rumor had it that he was one of the young white clergymen with John Lewis and other civil rights marchers when they were stopped and beaten by white thugs and law officers at the Pettus Bridge in Selma, Alabama, a protest that paved the way for the 1965 Voting Rights Act. It was said that Rev. Mike sustained permanent head injuries from that beating. Rev. Flowers doubted that rumor as well. Rev. Mike didn't impress her as someone who had participated in the old Civil Rights Movement. Besides, he didn't appear old enough. Rev. Brooks was of the same opinion, since he personally knew some of the old civil rights veterans, and none of them knew or had heard of Rev. Mike.

Rev. Flowers wondered why it was so hard for people, including herself, to accept that Rev. Mike was only a humble disciple doing what he could to please the Lord. She recalled what her father told her once about the price a principled person usually had to pay for sticking to his or her principles. "The higher the principles, the higher the price that society usually extracts," he told her, using Jesus Christ as a case in point. He then added, "Your grandfather believed this is why we must be leery of the wider world. He was a very rigid man in that regard."

****

Rev. Flowers stood in the open doorway of her office looking out onto the garden in the courtyard of the church. Standing there she noticed a large dove in the courtyard that appeared injured. It was having trouble getting aloft. Whenever it was about three or four feet above the ground, it would do a somersault and plummet hard to the ground. Then it would get to its feet and try to fly again, but would dive-bomb to the ground again. It was a wonder it didn't break its neck. Each time after failing to get off the ground, the poor bird would sadly look up at the roof of the building next door where it apparently wanted to go. Then it would try to get airborne again, but would fail again. It did this again and again. Then it dragged itself into the bushes and disappeared from sight.

"Poor thing! Its wing's broken!" Rev. Flower conjectured, horrified at watching a sentient creature that belonged in the air, but was unable to get up there. Her heart went out to the bird. What do you do about a wounded bird in your back yard? she thought. Do you call an animal shelter? She didn't know. She wished Rev. Mike was still around. He would know what to do about the bird. She recalled the time when he got the neighbor's cat down from the tree, which obviated the need to call the fire department.

While Rev. Flowers was fathoming what to do about the injured bird, Beulah, who must have been also watching from the kitchen, came out from her side of the courtyard and fetched the bird from the bushes and took it inside. Rev. Flowers didn't know what Beulah did with it after that, but was relieved that something was done. She disliked watching things suffer. She thought of the AIDS children in the hospital.

She laughed. The wounded dove made her think of the amusing story that Albert told about himself and pigeons. Albert hated pigeons. "Albert can see good even in the Devil, but not pigeons," Viola would laugh to friends.

One day she learned why he felt so negatively about pigeons. When he was about thirteen or fourteen years old he had an embarrassing mishap with a pigeon while on his way to a date with a girl he liked very much. It was the first date of his young life. While he stood all dressed up in his new suit and new shoes at the girl's front door with a bouquet of flowers, a pigeon crapped on him. Not once but twice. The first time on his shoulder, and the second time on his face when he looked up.

The girl's father opened the door before he could run away. When cute Margaret Ryan saw him standing there with gray and white stuff dripping off his face, he could've died. "That damn little pigeon did that just for spite," he would say when telling the story, pointing out jokingly that he didn't think it was a coincidence that the little pigeon was white. To this day Rev.

Flowers didn't know if the story was true or only something Albert had made up.

She spied a new Mercedes Benz pull into the parking lot. A tall lanky, well-dressed black man got out. Bright white teeth strode into the courtyard, and the teeth got whiter and brighter when the man saw her standing there. "I was just passing by, so I thought I'd stop and say hello, Rev. Flowers," he greeted her. There was a lively hop in his step that matched his big I-just-won-the-giant-lottery smile. The man was Rev. Jeremiah Shaw, Rev. Flowers' old friend. They went into Rev. Flowers' office so they could sit down and talk.

"I saw Rev. Scott in Memphis last week. We had a goodly crowd at the revival. He asked about you," he said with a little wink. Being an old friend, he knew that she and Rev. Scott had once been lovers. Rev. Shaw was a little envious of Manny Scott back then when he had a crush on Viola himself.

"Did Manny preach well?" she asked Jeremiah Shaw self-consciously. It was an unnecessary question because Rev. Scott always preached brilliantly, she thought.

"All night long he had them shouting to the heavens," Rev. Shaw chuckled. Turning serious, he asked her, "Are you going to the Midwest Gospel Conference next month?"

"I sure am," Rev. Flowers answered enthusiastically with a big smile, "I'm scheduled to preach at one of the sessions. I don't know which one yet."

Rev. Scott was also scheduled to preach at the conference, and being one of the hotshots featured at the event, his night had already been set and announced in the notices.

"So you've finally broken into the big time," Rev. Shaw laughed.

She returned the laughter good-naturedly, but his little dig hadn't escaped her. She knew he was being condescending. Preaching at the Midwest Conference was small potatoes to him. Rev. Jeremiah Shaw was a conservative black minister who preached to millions on television. Every Sunday on TV sets all over America he could be seen on the "Rapture Club" blasting the

Devil and Big Government almost interchangeably. The Rapture Club was a weekly two-hour syndicated television show of lesser-known conservative preachers modeled after Rev. Pat Robertson's fabled "The 700 Club." Often preachers on the Rapture Club show made minor guest appearances on the "700 Club" show, a program they saw as the big leagues.

Rev. Shaw told Rev. Flowers one day about the first time he appeared on the 700 Club, "The biggest thrill of my life was when the producers of the 700 Club called and invited me on their show to sing. It was like a gift from heaven." Rev. Shaw was referring to his magnificent baritone singing voice, a voice that was even better than Rev. Scott's powerful voice.

Rev. Flowers and Rev. Shaw started their respective churches around the same time. He started his in a rundown storefront in the Watts District of Los Angeles with a membership of about fifteen people, including his own family. For a long time he struggled to pay his storefront rent. He was so poor in those days that he bought his clothes, shoes, and even his underwear at the Salvation Army thrift shop. He built his church by personally going out Saturday nights and dragging back drunks from off the streets by promising them free sweet rolls and doughnuts. Because he allowed them to curl up in the pews afterwards and finish sleeping off their drunkenness, many of them stayed for church service the next morning. Many "found" God and joined his church.

His church grew and grew. Today it was one of the larger black churches in the city. Today Rev. Shaw's church, a grand spanking new structure on which they burned the mortgage six months after the large beautiful building was built, now had over five thousand members. Every year he drove a new Mercedes Benz that put Rev. Flowers' ten-year-old Volvo to shame.

A few years ago Rev. Shaw became involved with the white evangelical movement. Because of his enterprising nature and unwavering belief in America, he became enamored with the Christian Right. He saw America as the greatest country in the world, and a country in which anyone could get rich, even a black man. Since there weren't many blacks in that conservative circle, he felt very special. That specialness fed his natural cockiness. Thus the strut and the big Fuller Bush Man smile. Thus that firm handshake that made your hand numb after shaking hands with him. Thus that optimism that outshone the sun itself.

One day a white Christian friend introduced him to the stock market where he became a whiz. He became so adroit at picking stocks that his white friends regarded him as a genius. They gathered around him like disciples, which reminded Rev. Flowers of the way the white students used to flock around Manny Scott in their college days. Soon Rev. Shaw started his own stock investment club and newsletter. He then became a leader in the "Privatize Social Security" Movement.

It was through Rev. Shaw that Albert first became involved with the Republicans. It was Rev. Shaw who took him and Viola to the evangelical conference the night when Albert first met Bob Haines. Rev. Shaw then talked Albert into joining his Christian Stock Investment Club. After his first club meeting, Albert took Rev. Shaw aside and whispered, "Where are the other black folks, Rev. Shaw?" He was referring to the fact that he and Rev. Shaw were the only dark faces in the room.

"It's only you and me," Rev. Shaw replied, grinning proudly. He patted Albert on the back and said knowingly, "Too many black people seem to make white folks uncomfortable." He was hoping that good-natured Albert Flowers would agree with him that black people do better in the wider world when not tripping over one another.

It always amazed Rev. Flowers how money and success changed people. How it made them feel superior. Her old friend Jeremiah Shaw was no exception. Rev. Shaw now belonged to the "Jesus was a rich man" school of Christian theology, a theology that believed that God advocated the acquisition of wealth, and was very displeased with the laziness of the poor. Christian ministers who espoused this belief claimed Jesus taught that being poor was a sin, and that poorness was an avoidable curse in the Bible. The "Jesus was a rich man" preachers went so far as to say that if Jesus were on earth today, he would be living in a big expensive house, wearing designer clothes and jewelry, and driving a new Rolls Royce. Many of those ministers in their own lives did exactly that: they lived in big fancy homes, wore designer clothes and jewelry, and drove big fancy new cars, and were invariably conservatives.

Rev. Flowers eschewed that kind of thinking. To his credit, so did Manny Scott. They both believed that this "Jesus was a rich man" theology was a perversion of Jesus Christ's true teachings that the poor were the blessed ones, not the rich. That it was just another instance of conservatives twisting the facts to fit their beliefs. She and Manny believed that what displeased God most was a society that allowed people to suffer in poverty, and that this was what Jesus really taught, and it was this quality in Jesus that made her and Manny love him so.

Despite their theological differences, however, Viola Flowers and Rev. Shaw remained good friends.

"What do you think of the new organization that Brother Brooks is starting?" Rev. Shaw asked her. There was a demented twinkle in his eye. He knew that she and Rev. Reggie Brooks were good friends.

"I think the work he's doing with the AIDS children is wonderful. Praise the Lord. Those poor children need all the help they can get," Rev. Flowers said, proud of the young minister she had taught in Sunday school.

"I'm not talking about that. I'm talking about the group of homosexuals he's leading, who are trying to infiltrate the black ministry, like the white gays have done in the Catholic church," he said, darkening his tone considerably.

"Infiltrate? Reggie?" she said with an astonished look.

What Rev. Shaw just said seemed to come from left field, if not the moon. The charge was so ridiculous that it nearly knocked her off her feet. Then it occurred to her how nervous most male clergymen must be feeling presently because of all the sexual abuse scandals rocking the Roman Catholic Church. The newspapers, radio, and television stayed full of those awful stories. Stories that strongly intimated that not only were gay men more likely to be pedophiles, but that they had secretly infiltrated the Catholic Church.

She recalled the misgivings that Rev. Owens had about Rev. Brooks. He said with unbelievable gall that day, "Rev. Flowers, I just don't know about Brother Brooks. Some folks are saying he's a 'down-low' boy himself."

She shouldn't have let Rev. Owens's remark pass without comment, she realized now. Pass as just another instance of sour grapes due to Reggie's rapid rise as an important black religious leader.

She attempted to answer Rev. Shaw's ridiculous charge. "That isn't true, Rev. Shaw. Reggie's only trying to—."

At that moment her telephone rang, and as she reached to pick it up, Rev. Shaw handed her the large envelope he was carrying. "I gotta run, Vi. Give this to Albert. These are some stock performance charts I promised him." Before she could say anything more, he was gone, leaving her there cupping the phone. She had wanted to tell him that he was all wrong about her friend Rev. Brooks.

"Dear Jesus, please help Reggie. The Devil's busy trying to destroy him."

Chapter Twenty

"Albert, why are you home so early? Aren't you feeling well?" Rev. Flowers asked her husband when she entered the house. She had started worrying that he might be ill or something the moment she turned onto their block when returning home from a meeting downtown and saw Albert's car standing in their driveway at that time of day. Albert never took time off from work. When he worked for the county government, he received many awards and commendations for his attendance. She recalled how proud she was of him on the night of his retirement celebration when he received a plaque for his twenty-five years of service without missing a single day from work. That night she learned for the first time about all the many people he had helped over the years.

"You should be very proud of him, Rev. Flowers. Al's a damn good man. We're going to miss him terribly," was what she typically heard at the celebration. Many of his coworkers had tears in their eyes that night. One woman told her how Albert stood up for her when he was her union steward. "There weren't many blacks in our department. We had a prejudiced department chief who wouldn't promote blacks to higher positions. Although he'd smile in your face, he'd plot behind your back to keep you down. He didn't treat Mexicans any better. Even though I did the work of a top assistant, he wouldn't appoint me to the position when there was an opening."

"I thought County workers were under civil service?" Rev. Flowers asked her.

"We are. But he kept finding ways to get around the civil service laws and hire his white buddies from outside the department. It didn't matter to him that I was number one on the civil service list. Al had me file a grievance and he got the union to back me. We were able to prove both race and sex discrimination. We ended up getting that bigot fired. Would you believe it, Rev. Flowers, that Al discovered that this guy's girlfriend was his assistant department chief, and his nephew was the head of personnel. He was married too, with a wife and a slew of kids at home.

It all came out at the hearing. Your husband did a good job on my case. A real lawyer couldn't have done any better," the woman said gratefully. "Eventually I was offered the job, but Al got me transferred to even a better job."

That night at the celebration Rev. Flower heard many similar stories about Albert. It impressed her how well liked and respected he was by his fellow workers. Small wonder he always won his union elections by large margins.

When Viola entered the house from her meeting downtown, she found Albert sitting out on the patio, pale and visibly shaken. "Is there something wrong, honey?" she asked when he turned around and saw her standing there. He was so distraught that he didn't hear her when she entered the house.

He had the same horrified look he had that day a few years ago when the Internal Revenue Service padlocked his shuttle business for failure to pay employees' taxes. It was a day she would never forget. That day when Albert went to his office he saw his employees milling around in the yard like lost sheep. They should have been out on their runs, but their vans had been roped off by the IRS like a crime scene. Even the office was padlocked. There was an official notice on the door from the IRS advising of the tax levy. Albert was mortified.

It was not his fault. Bob Haines was in charge of preparing the payroll, and hadn't properly taken care of business. Because of a downturn in the economy, air travel was way down, adversely affecting the transportation businesses at the airports. Business was so bad that he and Bob Haines had trouble meeting the payroll; technically they were close to bankruptcy. Bob Haines went to their bank to increase their line of credit, but the bank refused them any more money, advising them to cut their expenses until business picked up, which of course would have meant letting some employees go. Bob Haines agreed with their banker. Albert disagreed. Being an old union man who believed that laying off employees should be their last recourse, he objected to their taking that drastic line of action.

"We don't need to lay anyone off. If we make layoffs, we probably won't be able to get them back when business picks up again. Good drivers are too hard to find," Albert argued strongly.

"What choice do we have, Al? We're damn near broke," Bob Haines pointed out in frustration.

"The worse is over," Albert answered," We can make it if we juggle a few things around for a little while." He didn't offer anything specific, but was confident that with all his good contacts Bob Haines could come up with something. It was Bob's job as CFO of the company to take care of such matters. He was like a magician when it came to raising money.

Bob Haines' face brightened. "I think I know where I can get some money to tide us over," he said, living up to Albert's expectations of him.

Albert gladly let him handle the problem, and stopped worrying about it. What he didn't realize at the time, however, was that Bob Haines would start monkeying around with the employees' withholding taxes to make ends meet. Then the economic downturn lasted longer than they anticipated. The hole Bob Haines was digging with the taxes kept getting deeper and deeper, while Albert went on doing his job innocently.

One day Albert discovered what Bob Haines was doing. He also learned that Bob had had many meetings with the IRS trying to clear up the matter. Then after numerous conferences with the IRS people, and after numerous broken promises to clear the account up, and after numerous official notices—and after a long silence that gave Bob Haines a false sense of things being OK—the tax people swooped down on their shuttle business like hungry hawks and seized everything in sight.

Albert was the first to discover the levy, and it frightened him shitless. He rushed home to guard his home, thinking his house might be next on the IRS's seizure list. At home he drew all the drapes and shades and barricaded himself in, and took a seat at the front window with the telephone in his lap. Had he owned a shotgun, it too would have been at his side. Then he called Bob Haines and their lawyer. Then he sat there by the window all afternoon trembling in his boots waiting for the feds, who never came because their lawyer successfully worked things out. By bedtime Albert was a psychological mess.

That was a few years ago. Now their shuttle business was doing fine.

Today Viola Flowers found him sitting there with that selfsame tormented look on his face.

"What's wrong, Albert?" she asked him again. She had kicked off her shoes because her tired feet were killing her. Her shoes lay askew on the kitchen floor like abandoned orphans. She had had a very busy day and longed for a short nap before preparing for religious services that evening.

"The FBI just left," Albert said, trembling, sweat dripping from his brow.

"The FBI?" she gasped.

He started to tell her what happened, then stopped, got slowly to his feet, and went into the kitchen where she joined him. They pulled out chairs at the kitchen table and sat down.

"Have you and Bob done something unlawful?" she asked him suspiciously.

"I don't think so," he replied wanly. "Most of the FBI's questions were about Bob and some other people I don't know." He got up stiffly and got himself some water and his hands shook as he lifted the glass to his parched lips. "The FBI had wanted to come to the office, but not knowing what it was all about, I had them meet me here. There's more privacy here," he said, kneading his fist nervously into his palm. "With all the drivers coming and going, I felt it would've been unwise to meet them at the office. It wouldn't have looked good to the employees."

"What has Bob done?" Viola Flowers asked gravely. She feared the FBI's investigation could be about anything since Bob Haines was into so much. It wasn't that she thought Bob Haines was a crook or anything. She knew he was a faithful husband, a loving father, a good citizen of the community, and a solid churchgoing Christian. It was only that, in her opinion, he was such a wheeler and dealer that anything could be possible. He always had many irons in the fire. Worse, he was a person who always took shortcuts to get things done, and who always looked for some advantage to get ahead. And it was like he believed the rules didn't apply to him. When he wanted something he was like a mouse after a piece of cheese for whom no hole was too small to get through. So it didn't really surprise her that the FBI was asking questions about him. She feared he might have gone too far this time and gotten Albert into trouble as well.

"Did the FBI say what they're were looking for?" she asked apprehensively.

"No. They just said they wanted to ask me a few questions about Bob. They kept asking me about people I hadn't heard of before." Albert removed his handkerchief and wiped his sweaty brow, groaning under his breath as he did so.

"What do *you think* they're looking for?"

"Who knows? Bob knows so many important people. You know Bob."

What worried Albert was that Bob Haines was always bragging about all his connections at the State Capitol in Sacramento and City Hall downtown. "With a little pull in Washington, DC, Al, we'll really be able to get big things done," he said when talking Albert into running for Congress.

Albert grimaced painfully as he recalled the state senator who went to prison last year from an FBI sting. Bob knew that senator. But what really worried Albert the most, though, were all the documents and papers he had signed with Bob Haines over the years on trust alone. So had Viola. His red-veined eyes got wider and redder as he agonized over it.

Rev. Flowers was thinking the same thing. Sitting there with a thousand fears percolating in her mind, she racked her brains trying to remember all the documents she had uncomfortably signed as Albert's wife in his many deals. She had their own lawyer check many of those documents, but that was the exception, not the rule. The rule was that most of the time she signed the papers placed in front of her on Albert's word alone that it was OK. Now shockingly she was learning that most of the time Albert had relied solely on Bob Haines' word.

"After the FBI left, I tried to call Bob but Alice said he was out on business somewhere," Albert said.

"Albert, do you think that was wise?" Viola Flowers made a sour face. Like most law-abiding citizens, the very thought of being investigated by the FBI made her very nervous.

"What do you mean?" he said with big eyes.

"Do you think it's wise to be talking to Bob about this matter. Especially on the phone. Maybe you should just stay out of it."

Stories about all the innocent people hurt in the President Bill Clinton /Whitewater investigation eddied in her mind. Many of those innocent people had their lives destroyed only because they knew or dealt with Bill or Hillary Clinton in some fashion. Rev. Flowers became angry whenever she recalled that most of the people cheering the Clinton attacks had been Republicans. Republicans like Bob Haines.

"Bob's my friend and business partner, Vi. I must talk to him."

"Then call Elder James first and see what he says," she urged him strongly.

When their discussion of Bob Haines was over, Vi disappeared into her study, leaving Albert at the kitchen table alone, where he sat with his head in his hands like someone with an awful migraine. Dark storm clouds had suddenly gathered over his once bright life and were threatening harsh rain and hail. Bob Haines' FBI investigation had cast a pall over everything the two of them were doing. Their business enterprises now stank like dog feces clumsily tracked in on the carpet. For a long while Albert remained at the kitchen table, pondering grimly what tomorrow would bring or possibly take away. "What's Bob done now?" he moaned over and over, shaking his head inconsolably.

Finally he pushed himself up heavily from the kitchen table and shuffled over to the telephone and called their family lawyer as Viola had suggested. Elder James wasn't in his office, so Albert left a message for him to call right away. Later that afternoon after spending all day in court, Elder James returned Albert's call. He had both Rev. Flowers and Albert get on the line.

"Do you think it's wise, Elder James, for Albert to be talking to Bob Haines while Bob's being investigated by the FBI?" Rev. Flowers asked, getting right to the point. "I realize that as business partners they must have some contact. I'm referring to any unnecessary contact that might pull Albert into this mess." She was thinking again of all the innocent people who were sucked into the Bill Clinton affair. She recalled how close Vernon Jordan came to being destroyed only because he was Bill Clinton's good friend. Jordan was a black man, and she remembered him from his days as president of the National Urban League when he used to speak at dinners she attended in Los Angeles.

"Vi, it's not against the law for me to talk to Bob. He's not only my partner but one of my closest friends," Albert interrupted pitifully on the other phone.

"You're right, Brother Flowers," Elder James said, "There's nothing in the law that prohibits you from talking to your business partner just because he's being investigated by the FBI. Just be careful about what you two talk about. It's all right to tell Mr. Haines that the FBI has been inquiring about him, but stay away from the matters you discussed with the authorities. Otherwise you might unwittingly become involved."

Elder James was thinking of wiretaps. He frowned and said, "Once a prosecutor goes on the rampage in a criminal investigation, no one's safe. Innocent people are often swept up in the investigation and then forced to accept guilty pleas to crimes they didn't commit, simply because they can't afford to defend themselves in court against more serious bogus charges. I know of numerous cases where prosecutors dug into innocent people's backgrounds to find minor crimes or something embarrassing to force them to give damaging information on the target of their investigation. This often places innocent people under enormous pressure to lie to avoid having their own lives ruined by trumped-up charges. So be careful, Brother Flowers."

As he listened, Albert Flowers peed his pants.

****

Because Albert had left word with Bob Haines' wife Alice that it was very important that Bob call him back immediately when he got home, Bob Haines called him the moment he walked into his house and learned that Albert had called. If Al Flowers said it was important, than Bob Haines knew it had to be important, because Al never bothered him with trifling matters. For if it was something he could do himself, Al would handle it. One of their drivers, for instance, had a heart attack one night after he had just left the airport with a van full of passengers. While driving north on Sepulveda Boulevard, he suddenly slumped unconscious over the steering wheel, causing the van to shoot out of control across the road, nearly hitting southbound traffic. It plowed into a sporting goods store, sending shards of plate glass in all directions. The accident killed three people in the van and a shoe customer in the store.

Upon being notified of the accident by the company dispatcher, Albert was at the scene immediately. In fact he was at the scene dealing with the police even before the ambulances arrived. He notified Bob Haines of the accident from the hospital, where after filling out all the police and insurance reports he had gone to check on their driver in intensive care.

"Do you need me there, Al?" Bob Haines asked him from the comfort of his home that night, reaching for his shoes.

"No. I think I took care of everything. Willie's on the critical list. All the other injured have been taken care of. I've called Willie's wife and she's on her way here now. You might want to drop by the hospital on your way to work tomorrow morning and check on Willie," Albert suggested.

"That's typical of the kind of self-sufficiency Al always brings to the job. Al never shirks from his responsibilities," Bob Haines would say proudly when telling his friends this story.

Hence today he gave Albert's urgent message his rapt attention. “What's up?” he asked when Albert pick up his phone before the first ring had finished.

“Bob, we must talk, and I don't want to do it on the telephone.”

“I'll be right there,” Bob Haines said, wondering what was up.

“No. I don't think we should talk here, either,” Albert said in a sinister tone.

“Then come over here. Alice just went to the mall and will be gone for awhile. We can talk in private here.” Now Bob Haines started to worry; whatever the problem was, it sounded very serious.

“I don't think that would be wise, either.”

Bob Haines flinched. Now he was really alarmed by Al's cloak-and-dagger behavior. It wasn't like Al to be dark and mysterious. This from a man who lived his life like a lit porch light. Bob Haines' heart began to pound even faster. They agreed to meet at a little bar called Louie’s Tavern which was about midpoint between their homes. They were careful on the phone not to identify the bar by name.

One might call the small neighborhood tavern a "white bar." Albert had been in Louie’s several times with a few of his white Kiwanis friends, but had never gone there alone. Although Louie’s Tavern was located in a racially mixed neighborhood of whites, blacks, Mexicans and Asians, Albert had never seen another person of color in there. There was no sign outside on the building or in the window telling the public that it was a bar. To most who walked past it every day, it looked like any other run-of-the-mill store front business. From its drab nondescript exterior it could have been anything from an old machine shop to a lawn mower repair business. In fact the little bar seemed to be hiding from unwelcome patronage in the neighborhood.

When Albert stepped into the little bar from the bright out-of-doors, it took awhile for his eyes to adjust to the semi-darkness of the place. He had never been in Louie’s during the middle of the day. The bar smelled of beer, buttered popcorn, hotdogs, and stale cigarette butts, and the crowd seemed different. When the front door opened and Albert entered, the laughter and chatter at the bar stopped, and all the steely white faces stared at the stockily built black man. At first those unfriendly faces made Albert feel like he had just stumbled unwittingly into a white supremacist hideaway. Then a friendly white male face behind the bar broke into a big smile. It was Gus the night bartender filling in for the daytime bartender who had to go to traffic court. Gus knew Al Flowers and his Kiwanis friends.

"Hi, Al. What are you doing here this time of day?"

"Hello Gus. I'm meeting Bob here. He's on his way."

Gus the bartender pointed to an empty stool at the bar. Since Gus knew Albert, the other whites in the bar accepted Albert and went merrily back to their chatting and drinking. Albert ordered a 7-Up after taking the stool next to two men talking about deep sea fishing. An old white woman on Albert's left was complaining about something to a man sitting next to her.

"It was one of the greatest mornings of fishing I've had in years. We caught a boatload of white sea bass, halibuts and red snappers," one of the fishermen said to his buddy, referring to the catch he had that morning at San Pedro. "I caught so much fish that I gave some to Louie for a fish fry here tonight." He then stood up on the foot rail and graciously announced to everyone in the bar, including Albert, that they all were invited to a fish fry tonight. "Everybody come tonight. The fish is free. Things should start around eight," he told them.

Someone bought him a beer.

The old woman at the bar was complaining to anyone who would listen about being laid off by a well-known department store in the Fox Hill Mall. "I didn't miss a day in over twenty years. I often came to work so sick that I was barely able to get out of bed. I went to work because I knew they needed me. And that's the appreciation I got. A goddamn pink slip," she said stiffly out one side of her mouth.

It was obvious that she recently had a stroke. The large blue veins in her forehead throbbed as she fussed, and in her mottled white hand was a beer, her third. Her fourth cigarette in the short time she had been there burned like a stinky incense in the ashtray at her elbow. The ashtray needed emptying.

"Annie, they probably let you go because you're getting too close to retirement. A couple of weeks ago 60 Minutes did a program on companies that were dumping their older employees to keep from paying them their retirement. They showed one man who was let go just a month before he was eligible to file for retirement. He sued the greedy bastards for age discrimination," a man said from the far end of the bar.

"I bet they let you go to make room for some nigger or Mexican under affirmative action. We white people don't have a chance anymore in this country," another man grumbled, who because he was in the men's room when Albert came in, hadn't realized a black man was in their midst and sitting with them at the bar. The other white faces at the bar turned red at the man's faux pas.

Albert pretended not to hear the racial remark. Dealing with white people as much as he did he had developed a thick skin against bigoted remarks like that. In his experience, he reasoned, most white people, even white friends, when dealing with black people will sooner or later let remarks like that slip out, usually innocently. "Racism is the snot in all white people's noses that will sometimes drip regardless of how many hankies they use," an old black coworker of Albert's was fond of saying on the subject.

Bob Haines' wife Alice was notorious for putting her foot in it. Albert recalled the first time Alice met Viola. The two women were talking about something that happened years ago in Los Angeles, whereupon Alice said, "Viola, you're probably too young to remember this, but—."

Rev. Flowers laughed that light laugh of hers and replied, "Too young to remember? Alice, you flatter me. I'm older than you are."

"How old are you?" Alice asked, thinking she was at least ten years Viola's senior.

Rev. Flowers told the white woman her age. Astonished Alice blurted out innocently, "You look so young, Viola. I'm always amazed at how *you people* don't show your age. Al's the same age as Bob, but you wouldn't know it. Al looks so much younger than Bob."

Viola was furious and gave Alice a piece of her mind. It wasn't Alice's comment about her age that upset her. It was her referring all night long to Albert and her as "you people." Viola hated that expression when used by white people when referring to black people. The only term she hated more was "nigger." Of course she later apologized to Alice for losing her temper, and they became good friends. Now the two couples often had dinner at each other's home, and they frequently attended each other's church. Bob and Alice Haines enjoyed services at the Church of God & Spirit mostly because of the lively music.

Regarding race, Viola and Albert were very different. Alice's remark would have bounced off Albert like water off a good raincoat. He would have moved the conversation on as though the remark had never happened. In his relations with whites he found this to be the best policy to avoid impediments.

The old cigarette lady at Louie's tried to make amends with Albert by showing him pictures of her grandchildren. Then to elicit his sympathy she told him about her stroke that nearly killed her after her layoff.

The front door opened. Bright sunlight again flooded that end of the dark bar, and out of that sunlight stepped Bob Haines, out of breath from hurrying to meet Al. He knew the bartender and most of the patrons in the bar. He took Albert around and formally introduced him as the candidate running for the U.S. Congress in their district. He distributed Albert's campaign literature as he asked for their votes, with Albert following him around shaking everybody's hand. The old cigarette lady lit up another cigarette and beamed, proud that she had just had a personal conversation with her future congressman.

Albert and Bob Haines then moved to a booth in the back of the room so they could talk in private. "The FBI was by the house this morning asking questions about you, Bob," Albert told him in almost a whisper after looking around first to make sure no one could hear them.

“Me?” Bob Haines eyes bulged like tennis balls. “The FBI? What did they want?” he asked nervously.

“I don't know. They didn't say. They only asked me questions.”

“What kinds of questions?”

Albert just sat there mum like a person sworn to secrecy.

“What did they ask you about me?” Bob Haines pressed him impatiently.

“My lawyer said it's all right for me to tell you that I was visited by the FBI and that they asked questions about you, but he advised me not to discuss the questions themselves with you,” Albert parsed his words carefully.

“Lawyer? What fucking lawyer?” Bob Haines snapped back like an angry turtle. Now he was really worried. If Al had to get legal advice in order to talk to him, then the situation had to be extremely serious. He broke into a cold sweat.

“Elder James, our family lawyer. After the FBI left, Vi thought it best that I check with him about the legalities involved in talking to you. You remember how all those people got into trouble with the Special Prosecutor just for talking to other people in President Clinton's case.”

Bob Haines' face shrunk, for he indeed did remember the Clinton investigation. Even though he was no Clinton lover and at first enjoyed seeing Bill and Hillary Clinton tormented by the Special Prosecutor, it reached a point where even he felt that the investigation had gone too far when it started hurting innocent people. He became really disgusted when the Special Prosecutor dumped all that salacious material on Bill Clinton onto the internet for the whole world to see. It was such an unchristian thing to do, he thought. This remembrance of the Clinton investigation made him all the more nervous about his situation.

Now he understood why Al became so nervous and consulted a lawyer. The FBI prowling around in his life sent chills up Bob Haines' spine. “Goddamnit! What a mess!” he shuddered to himself. Then taking a different tack, he looked Albert in the eye and said, “O.K., Al. I understand your predicament. I won't ask about the questions that the FBI asked you, but did they mention any names? At least you can tell me that."

Albert remained tight-lipped, but the involuntary reaction of his eyes told Bob Haines that the FBI had mentioned some names, which gave Bob something to work with.

"Did the name 'Lew Moon' come up?" he asked Albert, sounding like a questioner in a parlor game.

Bob Haines threw Lew Moon's name out there because it was the first name that came to mind of the people he had dealings with in the past who might be of interest to the FBI. He and Lew Moon used to be partners in a roofing business. He was the outside man who sold homeowners the new roofing, and Lew stayed in the office and took care of the paperwork. (This was before Bob Haines met Al Flowers.) Bob had no idea that Moon was a crook until long after their partnership had broken up.

A few years after their business dissolved, he learned that Lew Moon had defrauded many of their roofing customers, mostly old people, by falsifying their paperwork and applying for more money than needed for the roofing job, and pocketing the difference. Bob was lucky that Lew was never caught or else he might have been wrongly implicated. Was this why FBI agents were asking questions about him? Lew Moon? Now, after all those years? Bob thought.

Albert's mouth and eyes said nothing.

"What about Tom McCray?" Bob Haines asked next. Tom McCray was his well-connected friend who helped him and Al Flowers get their shuttle van business into the Los Angeles Airport. There was nothing shady about what McCray did for them, but Bob threw McCray's name out just in case. You never know about the FBI, he figured.

Albert's wide eyes showed surprise. He was puzzled why Bob Haines would think the FBI was investigating Tom. Did Bob know something about Tom that he didn't know? But he didn't dare ask Bob, so he remained silent.

"How about Saul Parry?" Bob Haines asked.

Saul Parry was the man Bob Haines and some friends hired a few years ago to help them get a zoning change for land they had optioned for a shopping mall they were planning. Saul Parry charged them a lot of money for his help. He called it a "fee," but due to the size of it they suspected that it was to pay off a certain city councilman to run interference for them. Although Bob Haines suspected that what they were doing might be illegal, he excused it on the grounds that all land developers did it. He and the guys even joked about it. As the grand leader of his lodge told him once: "If you're afraid to grease a few palms along the way, you'll never make any money in this world, Bob. Making money's not for the faint-hearted."

The shopping center was the biggest deal Bob Haines had ever attempted to pull off. His share of the land option and bribe money took every cent he and Alice had. The project failed when the city councilman reneged on the deal and demanded more money than they could raise. At least according to Saul Parry. It killed the deal. The guys in the deal, including Bob Haines, believed it was Saul Perry, not the councilman, who had tried to hold them up for more money. The failed deal nearly threw Bob and Alice into bankruptcy. The more Bob Haines thought about it, the more he was convinced that was the reason the FBI was investigating him. Just a few months ago some politicians in a small town south of them were arrested by the FBI for accepting bribes, and they were now awaiting trial.

"I can't answer that question, Bob?" Albert said about the name Saul Parry. But it didn't matter, for his sad unexpressive eyes had already told Bob Haines that it wasn't Parry.

"How about Asprey, John Asprey?" Bob Haines asked next.

Despite his sealed lips, Albert's eyes sprung alive like flicked cigarette lighters.

Bob Haines stiffened. Now he knew what the FBI was investigating. Of all the shady deals he had been involved in over the years, this one he feared the most. It was the only deal he definitely knew involved something criminal. A felony, in fact. John Asprey was an appraiser with the bank where Bob refinanced his house mortgage some years ago to raise $50,000 to pay his stock broker for his margin call. In his desperation and against his better judgment, he paid Asprey $5,000 under the table for an appraisal high enough to give him sufficient equity in his house for the loan, a serious crime under the law. Again he was told that everyone did it. Thank God that Alice knew nothing about it.

Bob Haines was now a ghostly white. He accepted the shot of whiskey that Albert offered to buy him and quickly downed it like badly needed medicine. Albert went to the bar and got him another one.

"Do you think I need a lawyer, Al?" he whimpered like a frightened child.

"I would if it was me," Albert answered sadly. Bob had boasted to him once about how John Asprey had helped him get the money, but he didn't go into the details, certainly nothing about the $5,000.

"Shit!" Bob Haines cursed aloud, for now he had a brand new worry. As tight as his finances were right now, where would he get money for a fucking lawyer? Then a third worry popped up and hit him like a sledge hammer. His wife Alice would now have to be told about Asprey. Then a fourth and more serious worry popped up. "Oh my God! Maybe Alice's involved as well, since she also signed those papers," he gulped painfully to himself.

"Perhaps it's all a mistake," Albert said sickly. He wanted to change the conversation, lest he might unwittingly step into forbidden territory, something he didn't want to do. He had learned too much already. Yet he wanted to comfort his friend. He didn't know what, if anything, Bob did that was wrong, but he could see Bob was visibly shaken up by Asprey's name.

"I hope you're right," Haines said, praying silently that all his fears were unfounded. He hoped the FBI was investigating John Asprey for something else.

"When it rains, it pours," he mumbled bitterly to himself when he remembered that Alice's car was acting up and probably needed a new transmission.

“Shit!” he cursed under this breath again as the two of them left Louie’s Tavern.

Chapter Twenty-one

"Thanks for inviting me over, Al," Bob Haines said as he stepped through the front door of the Flowers' residence. He was happy like someone just getting off probation. He grinned at Viola as he passed her to reach Albert. In truth he wanted to hug her for allowing him to come over.

Earlier that day he had called Al Flowers and told him that he had to see him right away. He suggested they meet at Louie's Tavern where they had been meeting secretly since learning about the FBI investigation. They had agreed that until the investigation was over they would keep their contact to a minimum and rearranged their work schedules in a way that kept them apart as much as possible. Bob Haines even took a leave of absence from Albert's congressional campaign until the smoke cleared.

When Albert told Viola that Bob Haines had called and that he had to go out to meet him, she replied, "Why are you two sneaking around meeting like common criminals? You two have done nothing wrong."

"We're just following Elder James' advice," Albert said meekly.

"Elder James only said that you and Bob should be careful of what you say to each other. I don't think he meant that you guys had to sneak around and meet like fugitives. Call Bob back and have him come over here," she said, annoyed by all their male foolishness.

However, she couldn't help being a little amused by the irony. During the Clinton investigation it galled her how their Republican friends, including Bob and Alice Haines, regaled in the Clintons' misery, and how they believed all the vicious rumors on the rightwing talk shows. The worst rumor was that Vince Foster, a top White House aide, was murdered by the Clintons, and that his body was hauled around for days in the trunk of Hillary's car. It seemed the more outlandish and scandalous the lies were, the more

Albert's Republican pals enjoyed them. Oh how they rejoiced when the Special Prosecutor made everybody in Bill Clinton's circle of friends squirm and sweat in fear of being pulled into that wide-ranging, ofttimes far afield, criminal investigation.

"Thank the Lord that Albert never joined them in all that nonsense," Viola Flowers said to herself back then. Before the Clinton investigation, even though she disagreed with much they politically stood for, Viola believed the Republicans were basically decent people, not the spiteful, lying people that surfaced during the Clinton affair. "How can people who claim to be born-again Christians be so vicious and uncharitable," she asked herself repeatedly during that sepulchral period. Maybe it should have pleased her that Bob Haines was now getting a dose of his own medicine, but it didn't, because he really wasn't a bad guy. Furthermore, her heart went out to his wife Alice.

Bob Haines was glad his exile was over. The separation had been very painful for both him and Al. Over the years since going into business together, they had become very close. He had really missed Al and their daily bull sessions. And Albert had missed him. Their dreaming and business strategizing together. It was always fun. He marveled at the working of Al's brilliant business mind that blended so well with his own. They were truly a team. He often said that Al Flowers was the best business partner he ever had. "Had Al and I met earlier, both of us would be sitting pretty by now," he would say, referring to the long line of crooked or inept partners he had gone into business with prior to meeting Al Flowers.

Getting their shuttle business started was very rough sledding at first, and at times the business appeared hopeless. But Al never despaired. He never lost faith that it would work, even when Bob Haines wanted to throw in the towel. "They're just bad bumps in the road, Bob. Our business plan's still sound. We must have the courage to stick with it," Albert would tell him whenever their business ran into difficulties. Albert was right. The shuttle business was doing fine now. It was doing so well in fact that they had branched out to other airports, and into other facets of the transportation business. Now for some ungodly reason the F.B.I. was in the picture.

"You guys go into the den and I'll bring you some coffee," Viola said, pleased by the satisfied look on Albert's round plump face. He was happy that his old sidekick was fully back in his life.

Rev. Flowers closed the door to the den and left the men to themselves. They were like two jubilant boys getting together again after both having been grounded. It had pained her to see Albert and Bob Haines suffer so. She realized, of course, that Bob Haines' difficulties weren't over. She was still very pessimistic about his fate. With all the balls Bob always had in the air at any given time, one couldn't be quite sure of him.

She bowed her head and said a prayer for him.

Chapter Twenty-two

Rev. Mike returned and pruned the church's fruit trees as he had promised, cleaning up and putting the branches in the containers to be picked up on trash day. He even pruned the roses. Rev. Flowers was rather surprised that he returned so soon, for usually it took him months, sometimes many months, to show up again. Her arms crossed, she stood in the doorway inspecting his work. Rev. Mike had done a good job. She appreciated how he cleaned up behind himself. The church garden was now even more beautiful.

She had about half an hour before her next appointment with Tara Henderson at 4:00 p.m. The Henderson girl was stopping by after school to consult with her about college. While she stood there enjoying the garden, the telephone rang in her office. It was her best friend Bernice, who was between customers and calling on a cigarette break from her beauty shop. In the background, customers could be heard laughing and talking.

Rev. Flowers always enjoyed Bernice's calls. Despite their differences about religion, for some reason she liked and trusted Bernice. There were few secrets between them. Their friendship was a strange one, she a gospel minister, and Bernice a nonbeliever who didn't believe in an afterlife.

"I believe when you're dead, you're dead," the high school dropout told Rev. Flowers earlier in their relationship.

Although Rev. Flowers' job was converting nonbelievers into believers, she never tried to convert Bernice because she knew better, and she liked Bernice exactly as she was. It was true that she, Viola, worried a great deal about Bernice's soul and prayed for her a lot. She particularly worried about Bernice's gambling habits. For Bernice's favorite pastime was playing the ponies everyday and going to Las Vegas when she could. She loved staying and gambling at Caesars Palace.

When being brutally honest with herself, Viola Flowers had to admit to herself that Bernice's irreverence was probably a big reason why she was so drawn to her. With Bernice there were never any moralistic judgments, just straight talk. More than with anyone else she knew, Viola felt perfectly safe telling Bernice personal things about herself. Things she wouldn't dare tell anyone else, not even her husband Albert or her sister Lettie. Things about herself almost too embarrassing for her ,to even think about. She even told Bernice about the time in Bible college when she thought she was pregnant with Manny's child, and actually thought about getting an abortion.

"When I learned later that I wasn't pregnant, I dropped to my knees and begged Jesus to forgive me for entertaining such a wicked notion. It took me quite awhile to get over that. For awhile I actually considered going into therapy.

That was the worst period of my life," she said sadly. She told Bernice that for a long time thereafter she refused to let Manny touch her sexually. She said embarrassed, "You're the only person I've ever told that to." Later that same day when back home and alone in her office, she couldn't believe she had told Bernice that, since she had sworn to herself never to reveal that to anyone.

Furthermore, Bernice was the only person who knew about the fear she experienced that morning when she came dangerously close to having breakfast alone with Rev. Scott in his hotel suite. "Truthfully, Bernice, I'm glad I didn't go," she told her hairdresser friend in confidence one day, "No telling what might've happened up there alone with Manny. God knows I love Albert very much, but Manny can bring the devil out in me like no one else can."

"I don't see the problem," Bernice deadpanned, "Just go ahead and go to bed with him, and get it out of your system. That's what I do when some handsome guy I'm attracted to is trying to get into my pants."

"Bernice, quit lying! You don't do that," Vi said, blushing like a rose, "You're always complaining about not having time for a love life." Viola couldn't help from laughing. Bernice could be so outrageous at time. That was another thing she liked about Bernice. Her bawdy frankness.

"Who's talking about love, girl," Bernice said seriously, "You got Albert for that."

Sometimes she told Bernice even darker things about herself, things she had heard for the first time spoken aloud, things that had lain in dark scary places inside her that she hadn't dared to explore on her own. Their friendship grew stronger over the years, and she and Bernice became soul companions.

She was pleased that Bernice had called. It had been a very busy morning and she needed a break. "What were you doing? Did I interrupt something?" Bernice asked in that devilish way she had of speaking where you weren't quite sure she was pulling your leg or speaking seriously.

"This was a good time to call. The tree man just left and my next appointment's not until four," Rev. Flowers said as she took a seat, put her feet up, and made herself comfortable.

"Girl, when we opened up this morning there was a long line of people waiting for us at the front door. This is my first cigarette break all day. My feet are killing me," Bernice said on the other end of the line. "I wonder what's happening in L.A. today? Why are all these black folks getting all spruced up? I know none of them are going to the Oscars Awards tonight," she joked.

"Maybe they're getting ready for church Sunday," Rev. Flowers said factiously.

"I doubt that," Bernice answered, "I don't think any of these folks are thinking about church."

"There used to be a time in L.A., though, when black folks got dressed up to go to church on Sundays," Rev. Flowers reminisced with sadness. She wasn't just thinking of Los Angeles. She had in mind black folks all over the country. In the old days Sundays were dress-up days for the black community. Days for church and big family meals.

Bernice said, "Mr. Bean says that in his barbershop in Watts in the old days his barbers stayed so busy on Fridays and Saturdays that they had to work way past midnight to get all their customers out. He says black folks used to line up all the way around the block to get all prettied up so they could go out partying on Central Avenue on Friday and Saturday nights.

He says Central Avenue really used to jump in those days, with a zillion jazz clubs where great musicians like Lionel Hampton, Buck Clayton, Big Jay McNeely, Buddy Collette, and Charlie Mingus played nightly. He says that almost every night you could see famous white movie stars in the clubs boogying with the black folks."

Mr. Bean was the old, semi-retired barber Freddie had hired to work the second chair on weekends. Mr. Bean once owned his own barbershop in the Watts District. In fact, his shop was quite popular at one time. "Go to Bean to get clean" was his business slogan in those days. Many of Rev. Flowers' older parishioners had once lived in Watts, which was then the main black community in Los Angeles. The old folks remembered how vibrant the community used to be, despite being very poor.

Those were the days just after World War II—the days when there were plenty of good-paying manufacturing jobs in the black community, the days when most black families had two parents, and the days when the black middle class still lived in Watts. Those were the days when the black community wasn't overrun with cheap handguns and drug dealers, and people had pride in their community, and those were the days when black folks, including the children, got haircuts, hairdos, shoe shines, wore hats, and dressed up and went to church on Sundays, with a big Sunday dinner afterwards.

"Those days are long gone," Rev. Flowers sighed, thinking of how the factories years ago packed up and moved to the suburbs, and then overseas. Of how the black middle-class left Watts to live in the newly racially integrated areas of the city, leaving poor blacks deserted on a desolated island of poverty and despair. "Now the Mexicans are moving in with their culture," she said in an uplifted tone.

After telling Rev. Flowers about her plans to go to Las Vegas next weekend, Bernice looked at the clock on the wall. "Girl, I gotta get back to that woman's head before she comes back here and drags me off this phone. I'll talk to you later. Maybe we can have lunch next week. Bye," Bernice said and then hung up.

In her mind's eye Rev. Flowers could see Bernice in those big floppy house slippers she always wore in the shop because regular shoes hurt her feet, scurrying back to a room of restive black women with their hair every-which-way.

There was a light rap on the frame of her open office door, and it was Rev. Flowers' 4:00 p.m. appointment, right on time. It was Tara Henderson, a teenage member of the church about to graduate from high school.

Watching the children of the church grow up was one of the delightful rewards Viola Flowers received for being a pastor. It was a wonderful thing watching them in Sunday school and getting glimpses of their hopes and dreams, and speculating on how their lives will turn out. Sometimes what she saw pleased her very much. But sometimes what she saw disturbed her deeply, because often the picture wasn't pretty.

She thought it was very unfair how some children seemed to have everything—nice homes with two caring parents, nice schools, nice clothes, and plenty of books and toys. Homes where television wasn't on constantly. Those children's futures seemed assured.

Then there were the children who had very little or nothing at all. Children who didn't have two caring parents. Children whose mothers were barely old enough or healthy enough to care for them properly. Children who didn't have nice schools. Children whose schools often had no books and were plagued with rats and other vermin. Children who had too much TV in their daily lives, and had no computers in their homes. Children who had to wear hand-me-down clothes or castoff things from thrift shops or public charities, and whose toys usually came from the same place as their clothes. Children who needed food stamps to stay alive. Children who were obese due to too much fast food.

All children Rev. Flowers knew would have to be both strong and lucky just to survive in life. They were mostly children whose difficult lives reflected what was happening or not happening in their parents' lives. It was so unfair, Rev. Flowers thought. "Where's the fairness, O Lord?" she would say to herself when thinking about those children.

Tara Henderson was one of the fortunate black children. Her future seemed assured.

"Hello Tara. Please come in and sat down. Are you just getting out of school for the day?" Rev. Flower said.

"Hi, Rev. Flowers. Thanks for seeing me." The girl took a seat in front of Rev. Flowers' desk. She was a pretty girl with big brown eyes and a chocolate face so expressive and cheerful that it made you cheerful just to look at it. It was a pretty face that was always smiling or always on the verge of smiling.

Rev. Flowers was very proud of Tara Henderson. Proud that she had stayed in school, stayed out of trouble, stayed away from drugs, and hadn't gotten pregnant like so many of the girls her age in the community. She was proud of Tara for getting good grades in school, and for planning to go to college. Proud of Tara for being the good role model that she was for the younger children in the church.

"What's on your mind, Tara?" Rev. Flowers asked when the girl had trouble getting started.

"Rev. Flowers, I'm graduating from high school next June, but my mother doesn't want me to go to college. She wants me to stay in Los Angeles and help with the business. I told her that I'd be more valuable to the business if I went to a good college and took courses in business administration. Then use that knowledge to help the business. Mama can only see the short term, not the long term. Would you talk to her for me?"

Tara helped her mother evenings after school in their small family business called Lulu's Pies, a small pie and coffee shop in the South-Central district that her mother opened up after the civil unrest in Los Angeles in 1992. After the Rodney King riot, many programs sprung up overnight to rebuild Los Angeles, which gave Tara's mother the opportunity to quit her job as a typist in a downtown office and pursue her dream of owning her own business. With her meager savings and a small government loan, she opened her pie and coffee shop. Tara was only a small child at the time. She grew up working in the pie shop. Many people regarded Lulu's pies as the best pies in L.A. and customers drove from as far away as Long Beach to buy them. Thanks to Albert's advice, some supermarkets started carrying them.

"Maybe your mother is afraid you'll go off to college and pursue other goals in life and leave her alone with the business," Rev. Flowers said as she thought of a Mexican family in her church that owned a small furniture refurbishing business who didn't want their children to follow them into the family business, not even the girls. They wanted them all to go to college. Like many immigrant families they wanted lofty professions for their children, not the drudgery, long hours, and low pay of a family business.

"She is. All Mama can think about is that I'll leave, get a college education, and then abandoned South-Central like so many college-educated blacks have done since the riots," Tara said.

"Well, will you?"

"Nooo! After college I want to return home and help grow the business. I've some good ideas. We educated African Americans shouldn't run from our old neighborhoods like we do. Land is too precious to do that. We should stay and help develop our community."

Then she looked at Rev. Flowers admiringly and said, "You always taught us that, Rev. Flowers. So has Mr. Flowers. You taught us that if something needs fixing, then it's our duty to help fix it. Remember?"

Hearing that made Rev. Flower feel good. It was the same thing that Reggie Brooks had told her. "Maybe the children are listening in Sunday school after all," she congratulated herself.

"I'll give your mother a call and talk to her," she assured the anxious teenager.

Chapter Twenty-three

"Albert, what would you think about us having another child?" Viola Flowers asked her husband one night at dinner. Wanting him in the right mood, she had prepared a nice dinner for the occasion, including sprucing up the table with flowers from her garden.

"A what?" He looked at her peculiarly. It was a strange question coming from a woman her age.

"A child. We have plenty of space here we never use. We have Maxine's old bedroom," she said sweetly.

"Children at our age?" Albert asked, thinking his wife had to be kidding.

"I don't mean that. I meant why don't we adopt a child. We have the room. There are so many children in the world today who need good homes," she said.

"Have you decided to be Junior Peterson's guardian?" Albert asked, knowing about Viola's conversation with Junior Peterson's grandmother awhile back. Back then he and Viola discussed the Peterson kid, where the idea of adoption came up. Yet as noble as the idea was, their adopting Junior Peterson bothered Albert. Where would they find time to raise the child? Viola was a very busy woman with a church to run, and he had a business to run, to say nothing of his new political career.

"I wasn't thinking of Junior Peterson exactly," Rev. Flowers said, then paused as though unsure of how she wanted to put it..

She wasn't speaking about Junior Peterson; instead she had the AIDS child in mind, whom she had been visiting regularly in the hospital. She had become very attached to the child. The "laying on hands" seemed to be working because on every visit the little girl appeared to be getting stronger, healthier. Then one day the child asked Rev. Flowers if she could live with her when she was well enough to go home.

"We'll see," was Rev. Flowers' noncommittal reply.

The child's question made sense. So for the rest of that afternoon the idea of adopting the little girl churned in Rev. Flowers' mind like cream in a butter maker. In fact even previous to that she had been thinking a great deal about adoptions generally, ever since Junior Peterson's grandmother asked her to look after Junior in the event of her death.

She resumed, "I was thinking about this sweet little girl I've been visiting in the hospital. I've told you about her. Every day she's getting better. It looks like she'll be getting out of the hospital soon. Her mother's dead, and she has no other family. She wants to live with us when she's released. What do you think, honey?"

"As I've said, Vi, if that's what you want, then it's all right with me. I guess we can work it out somehow," he replied, being nice old Albert and keeping his doubts to himself.

"Thank you, sweetie. I haven't decided yet what I'm going to do. I just wanted to get your approval first." She gave Albert a big kiss. His big heartedness was one of the main things she loved about him.

Rev. Scott then flashed in her mind. Often on important matters involving Albert, she would think of her old sweetheart Manny Scott and make comparisons. She would imagine what he would have done in that situation had she married him rather than Albert. Sometimes the comparison was favorable, sometimes not. This time it was invidious. Albert had gladly agreed to the adoption, whereas Manny would have found excuses why they couldn't do it. She recalled that evening at dinner when she told Manny about Junior Peterson, and the negative manner in which he responded. She had told him that Junior Peterson's grandmother had asked her to look after Junior if she died.

"Are you going to do it?" Manny asked her that night, frowning.

"I don't know. I haven't had a chance to talk it over with Albert."

"You're too soft, Viola. You've always been. You can't take in every little waif that needs a home," he said callously.

It was that very attitude that had contributed hugely to their breaking up. It wasn't that Manny disliked children. He loved children and was very good with them. And it wasn't that he was hardhearted or stingy. It was simply that, in her opinion, he just didn't have the right kind of heart to be a good Christian. He never had. Manny always had trouble understanding the true meaning of charity, even back in their Bible college days when they were dating. One semester he nearly flunked an important final exam due to that lack of understanding. He was asked by their professor in an essay test to define and explain charity in all its elements as found in certain verses of the Scriptures, and then provide appropriate examples. Manny correctly got the first two parts of the answer that their professor was looking for—1) the perfect love that Jesus has for us, and 2) the love we should have for Jesus. But Manny missed the third part of the answer which was: the love that God asks us to have for each other. Manny just didn't get it.

After the test Viola tried to explain to him why he had blown the question. "Manny, charity involves much more than just giving money to worthy causes like the American Red Cross. True Christian charity has little to do with money," she told him. "For Christians, charity isn't just a concept or a word to describe giving things to the needy. It's a way of being—a state of the heart, as the Apostle Paul would say—that we must develop from the teachings of Jesus Christ. We are commanded in John 13 to live life in a way that people will recognize us as Christians merely by the love and kindness that we show to others in our daily lives.

In other words, charity comes when we give of ourselves as Jesus gave of himself, his love, his service, his life. We must strive to give as Jesus gave." She was fussing at Manny Scott because of the "D" he received on the test. She had gotten an "A."

Back in their Bible college days Manny used to talk a lot about "heaven on earth." The only reason he believed in heaven on earth, she thought then, was to accommodate his own hedonism. His own materialism. In those days, every spare dollar Manny Scott could scrape together was used to put something on his back or in his mouth or to tickle his fancy. It wasn't that Manny was money crazy, for he wasn't. Nor was he enamored with the "Jesus was a rich man" approach to pasturing. That kind of thinking went too far, he thought. It was just that he liked the good life.

She and Manny always disagreed about the meaning of Matthew 16:27 and 28. She felt he hadn't given enough study and thought to such things as the judgment, the resurrection, the rapture, and other topics in the Bible pertaining to the final coming of Christ. Sometimes Manny lived like he didn't care about judgment day.

He hadn't changed much since then. Even today, with all his expensive cars, clothes, and exorbitant preaching fees, he still seemed not to have a clue. She felt that Manny was too self-absorbed to practice true Christian charity.

"Manny. Manny. Manny," she would moan hopelessly back when she was still in love with him.

****

After her discussion with Albert about little Elizabeth, Rev. Flowers got to her feet and went up to Maxine's old room to see what they would need if they decided to adopt the little girl. Through Maxine's window she watched the sinking sun paint the heavens with streaks of red and gold. A flock of ducks raced across the fading sky trying to settle in somewhere before nightfall. Flapping with all its might, a tired straggler was having trouble keeping up with the other ducks.

The straggling duck made Viola think of Maxine when she graduated from high school. For a long time Maxine seemed unable to get her life unstuck. She seemed not to know what to do with her life. Despite getting good grades in high school she never had any interest in going to college as her parents had wanted. She was unable to keep a steady job, and kept coming back home to live whenever she encountered financial difficulties. The last time was the third time she had U-hauled back home and reclaimed her old room. It wasn't that Maxine was lazy. On the contrary, she always worked. It was only that she kept hopping from one low entry-level job to another. Her life was like a pilotless motor boat going around and around on a small lake. For awhile Rev. Flowers feared Maxine might be on drugs.

"I don't know what we're going to do with that girl. She's so irresponsible," Rev. Flowers complained to Albert one day, "Mr. Burrell called me this afternoon and told me that she didn't show up for her interview." Viola was furious because Maxine had failed to keep a job interview at her bank that she had set up with the branch manager.

"Don't worry about Maxine, Vi. Like so many young people these days, she's trying to find herself," Albert tried to reassure his worried wife about their daughter.

Then almost miraculously Maxine got her life together when she fell madly in love with a job she was sent to by her temp agency. This assignment resulted in a permanent position, followed by promotion after promotion in the company. "I told you that she was just trying to find herself," Albert said to Viola proudly about the way their daughter had straightened her life out.

Viola Flowers sat up there alone in Maxine's rocking chair for quite awhile and pondered the grim things the doctor had told her about the little girl. The caseworker at the hospital told her that adopting little Elizabeth wouldn't be an easy matter, because the adoption proceedings might take court action since the little girl's biological mother was dead and there was no one else of record to sign the relinquishment papers. She also told Rev. Flowers that before she and Albert could start the adoption proceedings, they first had to qualify as foster parents, and that even though they were experienced parents, they would be expected to take a special foster-parent training course taught by an AIDS educator to make sure they fully appreciated what they were getting into.

"These children are cute and adorable, Rev. Flower, but they're very sick, and they require lots of care and attention. Most important, if you adopt one, you must be prepared for the fact that the child might die on you," the caseworker told her very bluntly.

Rev. Flowers told the caseworker that she fully appreciated the risk she would be taking. What she didn't tell the caseworker, though, was that she was "laying hands" on little Elizabeth, and it seemed to be working.

"The doctors have their work to do, and we have ours, don't we, Jesus," she would say to herself each time before ministering to the little girl. In her opinion, irrespective of what the doctors were saying, all their talk about white cell counts and antibodies notwithstanding, every day the little girl appeared to be getting better and better. Elizabeth's cheeks seemed rosier and her eyes seemed to dance whenever Rev. Flowers entered the room.

It wasn't that Rev. Flowers didn't trust doctors. She did. It was only that she believed prayer could help also. While she had no doubt that Jesus and his apostles performed miraculous healing feats in their time, she approached faith healing with great trepidation. She recalled all the ruckus in the media last year when a Christian family, because of their religion, went to court to stop the hospital and doctors from giving their ten-year-old daughter blood transfusions. The girl had been badly injured in a car accident. Rev. Flowers recalled seeing the father's press conference on television.

"We asked the judge to step in and save our daughter's soul. Jesus Christ is the supreme authority in our lives, and we will not let anybody make us disobey his commandments. In our religion, blood transfusions are banned by the Bible. Our daughter's in the hands of God now, and we know he'll do what's best for her," the father told reporters on the courthouse steps minutes after the injunction hearing. Regrettably, before the judge could render a decision, the daughter died. The girl's death raged all week on radio talk shows, and most of the callers blamed the parents.

Rev. Flowers agreed with the general public that the parents were wrong in blocking the blood transfusions. She didn't believe the Bible forbade all healing except through prayer. Her views on faith healing were like those of the Jehovah's Witnesses who, while practicing faith healing as a medical art, accepted most conventional medical treatments as well.

****

Because Viola had just come down from Maxine's old room, Albert sensed that she had been thinking all afternoon about Maxine. He saw the sadness on her face when she returned from upstairs. He knew how badly she yearned to be a grandmother and how savagely she had beaten herself up for their being grandchildless. How she blamed herself for Maxine's getting that botched abortion. How for months after it happened, she tossed fitfully in bed at night reproaching herself unmercifully for her bullheadedness that caused permanent damage to their teenage daughter.

He knew that she also blamed her sister Lettie for not telling her that Maxine was pregnant. "Had Lettie told me about Maxine's situation, maybe Maxine and I could've sat down and talked about it. Maybe I could've helped her make a better choice," she told him once in tears. When she said that to Albert that day, after hearing what she had just said it, she bemoaned painfully, "Choice? Did I just say choice? Dear Jesus, help me!" She admitted to Albert later that she found it impossible to think about what happened to Maxine without the word "choice" popping up in her mind. "Perhaps if Maxine had had more choices, by now we might be grandparents," she said to him.

Albert also knew that during those trying times Viola often got up in the middle of the night and went into her study and searched the Bible for stronger evidence that she had been right in her unyielding stand against abortions. Evidence that she was only doing God's will, but her biblical searches were futile. The Holy Scriptures now didn't seem as unequivocal as earlier readings.

"Please help me, Lord," he heard her beg God one night as she tried to reconcile the clashing texts in the Bible. In the thousands of hours she had studied the Bible over the years, he knew she had never wrestled harder trying to make sense of God's words. That during that dark period she spent much time down on her knees praying to the Lord to keep her strong. To keep her from straying as a good Christian. To help her understand Maxine's predicament without having to think about all the choices that might have produced a different result.

"There was only one choice, right, O Lord?" she asked many a night, sometimes in tears. Many nights she cried herself to sleep over what she did to poor Maxine and over the grandchildren they would now never have. "Please help me, God!" she would moan before breaking into tears again, before falling off to sleep. God never answered her. It was like he wanted her to figure it out for herself. At the time Albert was sure Viola was losing her mind. He even suggested that she see a psychiatrist. Those days were very hard for him as well.

Rev. Flowers eventually gave up trying to find an answer in the Bible. After all those horrible nights of spiritual and biblical searching, the only thing that made sense to her was that the decision about having an abortion was best left to the woman involved, just her, her doctor, and her God, because in the end only those three had any jurisdiction in the matter.

When Albert first learned of their daughter's abortion, it hurt him deeply that Maxine hadn't talked to him about her being pregnant, for she knew that his views on abortion weren't as rigid as her mother's. It was no secret that he was very ambivalent on the pro-choice versus pro-life issue. Even today a few of his Republican friends didn't fully trust him as a good "born again" Christian due to his shaky position on abortion. It was true, of course, that since he accepted the Republican nomination to Congress, on the advice of Bob Haines, his views were now more firmly pro-life.

"Albert has added some cornstarch to his pro-life views and stiffened them up a bit since he became a Republican," Lettie would jest about Albert's political conversion.

Chapter Twenty-four

Late one afternoon Rev. Flower received the shocking news from the hospital that little Elizabeth died. The child's weak little heart just stopped pumping, the doctors said. It was just that quick. One moment she was lying there smiling, the next moment she was dead. The news devastated Viola Flowers. She was totally unprepared for it. She had believed that her "laying on hands" was working. Rev. Brooks had warned her about getting too close to the child.

"In our line of work, Vi, we must love these children knowing that many of them will never leave here alive. We must love them for who they are *now* and the lives they have *now*. Many of them will have no tomorrow," he told her.

She marveled at how Rev. Brooks ministered to those poor sick children with such unflagging spirit. She wondered how he did it day after day. Where did he find all the strength? The energy? Her visits to the hospital always left her physically weak and emotionally drained, and she often had to take a long nap when she got home.

Upon receiving the news of the little girl's death, Rev. Flowers went into her office, closed the door, plopped down at her desk and cried her heart out. Tomorrow the painters were coming to paint Maxine's old room to get it ready for the little girl, and she and Albert had spent Wednesday evening at the paint store choosing the colors. Because little Elizabeth had spent most of her life on the AIDS ward, they chose bright colors that would cheer her up. Next week the store was delivering the new children's furniture Viola had purchased. And she and Albert were making good progress in the adoption process.

Now none of it would be necessary. Little Elizabeth wouldn't be coming.

As she sat there with her hands entwined solemnly on the desk, her face teary, Rev. Flowers glowered at the large picture of Jesus hanging across the room. Her visage was hard as ivory. "Why did you do it, Lord? Why did you lie to that little girl? She believed she had a tomorrow, but you lied to her. You lied!" she vented as she wept uncontrollably.

Jesus looked down at her as if to say: "I didn't lie to her, Reverend. You did. You're the one who told her that she had a tomorrow. You're the one who laid hands on her and pronounced her well. Not me. You're the one who led her to believe that she would be well enough to go home with you soon. I promised nothing."

He was speaking the truth. He had promised nothing. She was the one, not him, who had foolishly dreamed up a future for that poor sick child.

"Please forgive me, Jesus," she wept piteously, feeling shame for falsely accusing him. For disrespecting him. She was an emotional wreck.

When she eventually pulled herself together, her office was in complete darkness. "Oh my, where did the time go? I have services in an hour," she moaned, looking at the clock before getting to her feet. She really didn't want to face the congregation tonight. She felt like a fraud. There had been other days in her professional life when she felt like that: days when she wanted to take her certificates down from her office wall and burn them. Days when she wanted to take her ministerial frock off and burn it as well. But today was the worst day ever. She sorely feared she was losing her faith, if not her mind.

"Please, Jesus, go out there with me. Please take my hand. I don't have the strength to do it alone," she asked as she went into the bathroom to clean herself up.

****

A few days later she officiated at the child's funeral. Remembering that God promises nothing, especially to children, she did what she could from the pulpit to help get that beautiful little coffined child into heaven.

****

As if losing that sweet child wasn't bad enough, in two days she had to leave for an intergospel convention in St. Louis, where many of the nation's leading gospel ministers would be preaching, including Rev. Emanuel Scott. She hadn't spoken to Manny since that morning when she had to cancel their breakfast engagement because of the flat tire. She didn't want to see him, especially right now in her very vulnerable state, but there was no way she could avoid seeing him at the convention. Her heart began to throb and her hands began to shake.

"Easy, girl. Calm down. You have handled Manny many times before. Just remember, it's been over between you two for a long while now. So keep it that way," she lectured herself sternly.

Chapter Twenty-five

The Lantern Book Store on Pico Boulevard was Rev. Flowers' favorite Christian book store. She enjoyed stopping there and browsing through all the new books she would like to read if she had the time. She particularly enjoyed memoirs by early women ministers and found them very inspiring. She could relate to what they all had to contend with in trying to break through the male-dominated structure of their various churches. Lately the store had begun carrying a few books on the lives of black churchwomen.

Wandering through the book store reminded her of when as a small girl she used to go to the public library with her father. At the time Lettie was too young to go with them. Young Viola even had her own library card. "Take good care of this. It's very valuable," her father said when he handed her the card after the librarian had typed it out and handed it to him. Viola was very proud of that little card with her name on it, and felt very grown up when her father allowed her to keep custody of it after she promised him that she wouldn't lose it. Her library card was the first real thing of value that she put in her little shoulder purse that she always wore when dressed up. It boggled her young mind the way she and her father could check out any book in the library that they wanted, free of charge, merely by handing the woman at the checkout desk their cards. It was like waving a magical wand, young Viola Flowers thought. For her, the public library was a wonderland.

As she stood in the aisle of Lantern Book Store fingering through a book that had caught her eye, a familiar voice said from behind her, "That's a wonderful book. You must read it." She turned and there stood Rev. Evelyn Bowman, Rev. Brooks' minister friend she met that night at Rev. Brooks' big meeting that ended in such a disaster.

"Hello, Rev. Bowman. How have you been?"

The two women exchanged greetings.

“She's a good writer. Have you read her other books? They're very good. She's also an expert on the theology of dying,” Evelyn Bowman said about the author of the book that Rev. Flowers was holding. “She believes that one is not prepared to live until one is prepared to die. She shows how death fits into God's grand mosaic for the universe. She says that everything in the world is regulated by death. The planets in the heavens, the trees in the forests, the birds in the trees, as well as we humans on the ground. She's very deep. I saw her on Oprah once.”

The two women stood and chatted awhile about the book, which Rev. Flowers ended up buying. Then she and Rev. Bowman moved to the cashier at the front of the store.

“Would you join me for a cup of coffee, Rev. Flowers,” the young minister asked, referring to the coffee shop next door. “I would love to,” Viola replied after glancing at the clock to see if she had enough time.

When they stepped out into the bright daylight, Rev. Flowers saw that Rev. Bowman was even younger and prettier than she remembered from their first meeting that night at Rev. Brooks' church. There was a certain smartness about her that was very striking. Rev. Flowers had heard about the good work that Rev. Bowman was doing at Calvary Baptist. As she did with respect to all female ministers, Rev. Flowers took delight in Rev. Bowman's success as a pastor. Because of all the struggles, hardships, and sacrifices that women had to endure to achieve leadership roles in most churches due to sexism, she always felt proud when any woman pastor, irrespective of domination or faith, achieved in her ministry, for it showed that women can do the job as well as men.

In the coffee shop they took a table by the window. After talking awhile about the problems that both of their churches were having with their general giving, Rev. Bowman said on a more positive note, “This Friday we're having a special fundraiser to raise money for our new baptistery.” She went on to tell Rev. Flowers about how cute the small children were at their baptism last week.

Their conversation about baptisms made Rev. Flowers very sad as she recalled the first baptism she ever witnessed. She couldn't have been more than four or five years old at the time. She recalled it like it occurred only yesterday. It was a warm summer day in Iowa where they lived at the time. The baptism was in the river. Very few black gospel churches in those days could afford baptisteries. That day the women were all dressed up in long white frocks, while the men wore white shirts, black ties, and black trousers. Parishioners flocked on the river bank like birds to watch the ceremony. It was like a big family picnic. Little Viola and her family stood on the bank with other families watching church members wade out into the river to get baptized. Her father and some male parishioners stood thigh high in the water and baptized members by dunking them like doughnuts into the river, causing some to kick and giggle. To the kids, it was both fun and scary.

Then there was a piercing scream from one of the mothers whose small son had fallen into the river and disappeared. The baptisms stopped and everyone joined in the search for the little boy. The sheriff arrived with his deputies and they dragged the river. And they still hadn't found the little boy when Viola went home that afternoon. That night before climbing into bed, she and her mother said a prayer for the boy. "He was selected by God to be an angel to the little fishes," her mother told Viola to console her before tucking her in for the night.

That night little Viola dreamed about the little boy's being up in heaven protecting God's little water creatures. The boy's body was recovered three days later in the Mississippi River. Their church stopped baptizing in the river that year because of the danger. Also many parishioners thought using the river was too old fashioned.

Rev. Bowman pushed her coffee cup to one side. "What a lucky coincidence it was that we bumped into each other in the bookstore. Rev. Brooks asked me to work with Bishop Neely in setting up the next big meeting of the black ministers. Bishop Neely suggested that a small group of us should meet first to work out some goals and strategies to recommend to the main group. He feels that if we can hit the ground running, we'll have a better chance to avoid disruption by the dissenters.

She added, "He thinks in the long run we can make better progress that way. He feels that failing to plan is planning to fail. He asked me to run the idea by you first. He and I both agree that whatever our strategies are, getting the total black religious community involved in the fight against HIV/AIDS must be our main goal."

"Me?" Rev. Flowers said with wide eyes, pointing to herself, wondering why they had included her. She wasn't a part of Rev. Reggie Brooks' group. She was just Reggie's good friend. Like with the other pastors that night, she had attended that first meeting only because of Reggie's public service announcement. Apparently she had failed that day in Bishop Neely's bedroom to make it clear to him that she was not a part of Reggie's group, and that before the night of the big meeting she knew hardly anything about his project. Events were taking her in a direction that she didn't exactly want to go, and she didn't like it. She recalled the circus parade long ago that got her into trouble with her mother. True, she had sympathy for what Rev. Brooks was trying to do. How could she not have sympathy. Each year millions of AIDS victims were dying around the world. And she would never forget poor little Elizabeth. But being a leader in Rev. Brooks' group was another matter entirely.

She recalled what one preacher who walked out of Rev. Brooks' meeting that night told her a week or so later that disturbed her very much. "We must be very careful these days, Rev. Flowers. We don't want the gay black preachers doing to the black Protestant Church what the gay white priests are doing to the Catholic Church. We don't need a mess like that," he said.

Then he accused Rev. Brooks of trying to set up a front organization of homosexuals so they could take over leadership of the Black Church. That horrendous charge nearly knocked Viola Flowers off her feet. The accusation was so ridiculous that she didn't even bother to argue with him. She knew Reggie had no such agenda. Besides, Reggie wasn't gay as far as she knew.

Before Rev. Flowers could reply to Rev. Evelyn Bowman in the coffee shop, the latter added, chuckling, "Truthfully, I think Bishop Neely would like you to chair this committee, but knowing how busy you must be with your radio show and all, he's reluctant to ask you."

Rev. Flowers sat there speechless for a few seconds, then said feebly, "I'll have to think about it, Rev. Bowman."

She had chickened out again. She should have come right out and flatly told Rev. Bowman "no." She should have told her the truth that due to her views on homosexuality, she didn't want to get involved anymore than she already was. But she didn't. She was too conflicted. Conflicted because there was a part of her that wanted to be involved in Reggie's project.

"Its black preachers like yourself who are compounding the problem," her conscience told her day after day. How does the old saying go: If you're not a part of the solution, then you're a part of the problem. That was what her conscience told her, making her feel very ashamed of herself. All the while, this feeling clashed with her religious beliefs that opposed homosexuality. Like in a rough game of tug of war, her religious beliefs were pulling her just as forcefully in the other direction.

So instead of telling Rev. Bowman the truth, she told her a half-truth: that she was very busy preparing to go to a religious conference in Missouri and couldn't give her an answer until after she returned. The truthful part of her statement was that she was in fact going to a conference out of town. The less than truthful part was that she already knew her answer, which was: "No, thank you. I want no part of what you guys are doing."

"I'll call you when I get back," she equivocated uncomfortably.

At that Rev. Bowman got to her feet and said she had to run. "Bishop Neely said you might not have the time. Please call me as soon as you can and let me know?" she said.

"Yes, of course," Rev. Flowers said weakly, getting up also, feeling lousy for wimping out again.

Outside the two women moved off in opposite directions to their parked cars. Rev. Flowers stopped suddenly and hurried back to the coffee shop. She had left her book purchase on the table.

****

Back at her office Rev. Flowers was disappointed in herself for not telling Evelyn Bowman that she was not a part of Rev. Brooks' organizing effort, and had never been. Bishop Neely had just assumed she was one of Rev. Brooks' lieutenants, which was not the case. Far from it. Rev. Reggie Brooks was only an old friend that she had helped to publicize his first meeting. Nothing more. The misunderstanding was her own fault, she felt, because she should have made her position perfectly clear to Bishop Neely that day in his bedroom. And she should have spoken up today in the coffee shop as well.

The truth was that she was extremely flattered that Bishop Neely had summoned her to his home that day. She hadn't realized prior to that day that Bishop Neely regarded her so highly—she, the pastor of a small gospel church. His respect meant much to her. As a female minister in the holiness tradition, she had always had to fight for respect from the more mainstream churchmen. It was a constant struggle just to be taken seriously.

Most Church of God & Spirit churches deliberately limited their contact with mainstream churches. Even her more enlightened father kept the national church off to one side away from the dangerous mainstream Christian thinking of his day. She was the first pastor in the history of her church to have regular relations with Presbyterian, Episcopalian, Unitarian, Lutheran, Methodist, Baptist, and even Catholic churches. She attended many interdenominational conferences. Her instincts told her that this was the right thing to do. She always held her head high, proud of her small gospel church.

Now her pride had gotten her into trouble. She had let her pride tie her tongue, which in turn resulted in false assumptions by others who trusted her. She should have told them that while they had her prayers in their effort, she couldn't join them because of her church's opposition to homosexuality. A sermon she gave once about pride being the origin of all sin came to mind. She recalled Philippians 2:3 of the Bible that admonishes against letting pride be your guide when you're doing something. She felt miserable about misleading Rev. Bowman and Bishop Neely because of her pride.

Feeling she needed to pray, Viola Flowers got down on her knees with fingers tented. "Please, dear Father, humble me. Please rid me of all this pride I have inside of me, and bring me back to the humility and grace I had when I first accepted you as my Lord and Savior. Please cleanse me of my prideful ways. Please help me be a better servant of thee. Please forgive me. I ask all of this in Jesus' name. Amen."

Upon opening her eyes she saw her grandfather in the photograph looking down at her sternly. His hard-boiled expression appeared to be chiding her for getting involved with those supporters of the homosexual lifestyle. His cutting look reminded her of the look her father gave her once when her mother scolded her as a teenager for going to the movies with some friends after a friend's birthday party. It didn't matter that the cinema and the popcorn had been a gift to all the girls at the birthday party from one of the parents. She was scolded anyway because she knew that going to the movies was against her religion. Even though she was truthful about where she had been, she was nonetheless punished when she got home. "Viola, shame on you! You of all people, disobeying God's commandment like that! Now go to your room, get down on your knees, and ask God's forgiveness," her mother rebuked her angrily. Her father just stood there in silence, with deep disappointment on his face. He had that selfsame look that her grandfather had now in the picture.

"Would I be doing wrong to help them, Grandpa?" she asked the distinguished old black gentleman in the photograph, the man who was her idol and role model. The question seemed needless, but she had to ask it.

Her church, going back to her grandfather's days, had always been very parochial and seldom collaborated with other religious organizations. From the very beginning, her grandfather taught his flock not to wander too far a field because the secular world was a dangerous place for real God-fearing people like them. He saw the secular world as mostly a place wickedness. He saw other Christian churches as mere pawns of that wicked world.

"We Church of God & Spirit followers should take a lesson from the Amish people. The Amish don't allow outsiders to track the dirt of the world into their lives," he would say when speaking to his parishioners about why they should be wary of outsiders. He admired the Amish, a small religious group who broke away from their strict Mennonite life in Europe hundreds of years ago so they could live an even stricter religious life in the United States and Canada.

This kind of thinking was also true in Rev. Flowers' father's time, even though her father sometimes felt hemmed in by the conservatism of the Church. "Sometimes I think we gospel folks are too straight-laced and stodgy," he admitted to Viola one day.

When she got her own church going, Rev. Viola Flowers started venturing out more. "We can't keep hiding from the rest of the religious world," she told her skeptical board of trustees the first time she asked for money to attend an interdenominational conference in Chicago. "It's time we start trusting ourselves and join in fellowship with other Christian churches," she told them.

That was a drastic departure from the policy of her father and grandfather. She had changed considerably since her college days. Back then she and Manny Scott often had heated arguments about how involved gospel churches should be with the secular world. Manny Scott was more liberal than she was. He used to argue with good humor, "Jesus believed in heaven on earth, not pie in the sky. That's what's wrong with you Church of God & Spirit folks. You got your silly heads up in the clouds. You guys are almost as bad as we Church of God & Christ folks, and we're pretty bad."

It wasn't surprising, therefore, that after Bible college Manny left the Church of God & Christ for a more open-minded gospel church. Manny's remarks used to bring tears to Viola's eyes, and many times she came close to accusing him of blasphemy.

Chapter Twenty-six

The day before Rev. Flowers was to leave for St. Louis, she got more bad news. Her radio show was canceled, which was the longest running religious radio show of its kind in Southern California. A creature born of desperation, the gospel radio show itself stemmed from the Watts Riots in 1965, at the apex of the Civil Rights Movement when African Americans were sick and tired of being second-class citizens and began protesting all over America. Race riots rocked the country, and Los Angeles was no exception.

For six days blacks torched and looted the Negro community of Watts. Many people were killed. On the first day of the riots, the white radio station manager at KWCP invited black leaders, particularly leading black preachers, to come into the station and go on the air to help quell the racial disturbance. One of the pastors who responded to that call was Sister Eva Carrie from Temple Baptist Church. While Watts burned, she spun gospel records everyday in her radio booth at KWCP, and prayed on the air round the clock for the black people of Watts to come to their senses.

She begged the young men roaming the streets to return to their homes and help build their community, not destroy it. Many of those young men heeded her plea and got off the streets. Sister Carrie became so popular in South-Central Los Angeles that the radio station gave her a weekly gospel show that ran for years until she suddenly dropped dead one day from a heart attack.

Rev. Flowers took over that radio show, and its success continued to grow. Under her, the radio show became famous for its great gospel music, its religious public service announcements, and its sincere over-the-air prayers for the sick, the shut-ins, and the homeless. Rev. Flowers even prayed for men and women in prison. In fact prayer was there for anyone who called in and requested it.

Today Viola Flowers received a telephone call from the station's program director telling her that her show had been cancelled. "Why, Larry? Why did they cancel my show? I thought my ratings were good?" she asked him, nonplussed. The news was shocking because a sizable number of African Americans in Los Angeles liked and listened to her show.

The main reason the news was so surprising was that good programming, not necessarily high ratings, was what mattered at KWCP. Thanks to the station's maverick owner Harry Bordwell, who poof-poofed Arbitron ratings, KWCP never joined in the mad race like other radio stations did for larger and larger audiences at whatever cost to good programming.

"I bought and built this station up from scratch. I don't need some high-priced consultant telling me how to run it. It's mine. I know what my listeners like," Mr. Bordwell would say pigheadedly when anyone, including his accountants, tried to tell him that his station was underperforming in terms of profitability. He and Rev. Flowers were very good friends, and he was an ardent fan of her show.

Because Mr. Bordwell always backed his programmers, he was beloved by everyone at the station. He always gave his programmers the freedom to be bold and creative, which was why they loved and respected him so. Then he fell seriously ill and had to be hospitalized.

Now upon receiving news of her cancellation, Rev. Flowers felt she had let Mr. Bordwell down somehow.

"It's not your ratings, Rev. Flowers. Your ratings are fine," the program director said on the other end of the phone. "The station's being sold. The station's changing its format and letting everyone go," he said grimly.

"Has Harry taken a turn for the worse?" Rev. Flowers asked with alarm, referring to the sick owner. True to her kind and tender nature, her first concern was Mr. Bordwell's health. For her, the format change and her pink slip were secondary. She knew it had to be something very serious to make Mr. Bordwell sell the station.

For years the big media giants had been trying to buy KWCP, but Mr. Bordwell refused to sell it.

Last year after a couple of disappointed men in expensive suits and highly polished oxfords left his office, Harry Bordwell told his staff, "Those Wall Street morons want to make me a multimillionaire for a piece of junk I picked up a few decades ago for just a few thousand dollars because no one else wanted the station. I told them to shove it. I'm not letting them turn this radio station into a haven for mean rightwing talk shows."

To Rev. Flowers' question about Mr. Bordwell's health, the program director replied dryly, "No, Harry's about the same. But it doesn't look good. His oldest daughter Dorothy says the family must sell the station because they badly need the money to pay all the medical bills that are piling up."

"Who's the new owner?" Rev. Flowers asked, figuring the new owner was Clarity Bell Broadcasting System, a huge media company well known for buying up stations. Prior to media deregulation in the 1990s, Clarity Bell owned only 30 stations nationwide, but now it owned over 1,500 radio and television stations, and more than 500,000 outdoor billboards worldwide.

Many of the musical groups that visited KWCP on tour often complained to Rev. Flowers about how hard it was now to get their music played on the air. "Now just a handful of corporations own everything, and they're shutting out independent artists and producers. Before deregulation there were many stations that would play our music, but they're not around anymore" a frustrated leader of a black musical group told her one day when they visited KWCP promoting their new CD.

Rev. Flowers learned the musical group was having trouble getting airplay because many of their songs had anti-corporate themes.

Regarding Rev. Flowers' question about the identity of the new owners, the program director answered, "I don't know. I've been dealing with a representative of the investment group involved."

"Are they changing to Top 40?" she asked.

Rev. Flowers was referring to the fact that KWCP was far from a top-40 radio station. KWCP was a very creative, eclectic, and deeply community-involved radio station. The station had won many news and music awards. Its popular public affairs director was an active player in the African American community, providing leadership and resources to many neighborhood activities, such as fundraising for Sickle Cell and summer camps for disadvantaged children. The station's talk shows were always fair, civil and informative, with no screaming, shouting or hatemongering. The music programmers were always free to select and play their own music, which most of them did, often bringing in their own records and CDs to play. No Top 40 for them. It was obligatory for touring musical artists to make appearances at the station when performing in Southern California.

"Who knows and who cares," the program director replied sourly to Rev. Flowers' Top 40 question.

"What's wrong, Larry?" Rev. Flowers asked after sensing bitterness in his voice. She wondered why he was spending so much time on the phone with her when he had all those other termination notices to deliver. He had told her that his telephone call to her would be confirmed by e-mail or fax, followed by a special delivery letter. "With all the work he has to do after we hang up, why is he lingering?" she wondered.

After an intense silence, he said brokenly, "I think before the day's over, I'll be fired too. They're letting everyone go."

"Do you want me to say a prayer for you, Larry?"

"Yes. Would you please," he said in a sick voice.

Her prayer for the program director was just the first of the many she made for station staffers who called her over the course of the day and asked for prayers, some in tears. It was like they thought she had some special pull with God. She had no special pull with God. She had received a pink slip along with the rest of them. Sister Lorraine, for instance, the longtime host of The Lorraine Madison Show, was so distraught about losing her job that she didn't want to hang up. She hung on to Rev. Flowers like someone hanging on for dear life to a tree branch out over a deep gorge. She stayed on the line with Rev. Flowers for over an hour before letting her go.

"My, what a mess!" Viola Flowers, now with a splitting headache, said to herself about what was happening at her beloved radio station.

****

Early that evening Viola Flowers repaired to her study and got down on her knees and prayed. The Lord told her to reexamine the important things in her life, and then make adjustments. He was speaking of her losing her radio show. Hence she summoned Albert into the living room, and the two of them discussed the cancellation of her show. She told him about how shocked everyone at the station was by the news, and how devastated they were to suddenly find themselves unemployed. Every day with fewer and fewer people needed in radio broadcasting, good radio jobs were now very scarce, she told Albert. Telling him that her friends at KWCP were scared to death that they would never work in radio again, or if they did manage to stay in radio, they would have to move to another city to do so.

Because her show was so popular in Los Angeles, Viola Flowers was hopeful she could find another local station for her radio show.

****

Feeling they needed a backup plan in case she couldn't get another local radio show, Rev. Flowers and Albert sat down again that night to talk about the belt-tightening they now had to do concerning their family budget. As a family they would miss Viola's radio salary, which, while not very large, gave them the extra money for the few luxuries they did enjoy in life. When they finished their new budget, Viola remarked that tomorrow she would make some phone calls around town to see if she could find another radio station that would take her show which was very popular in Los Angeles. In the past other radio stations were always trying to steal her from KWCP.

"That won't be necessary, Vi," Albert said, meaning her radio job search. "This might be a blessing in disguise. You need to slow down some. You work too hard. I can handle things financially." He meant his salary from his shuttle business which was now making a nice profit.

Viola wasn't convinced; she disliked having to depend on Albert's income. It was too iffy. His and Bob Haines' wages were the thermostats that were always being adjusted up and down to keep their company's books balanced. Even worse, she never knew when he and Bob Haines would embark upon another risky business venture. When it came to "get-rich-quick" schemes, those two were as unpredictable as two yard dogs addicted to car chasing. If the gate was open, they were gone, yelping.

The telephone rang and Albert answered it. He blanched, then he looked at Vi with a downcast expression. "It's Bob. He wants to come over," he told her warily.

"Didn't you tell him that we're very busy right now?" Viola said with annoyance. She was annoyed at Albert for not telling Bob Haines to call back later, something she would've done had it been her friend calling at such an inopportune time. She and Albert hadn't finished their family matters. This was another instance of Albert's always putting business matters before family affairs.

"Bob says it's very important," Albert said meekly.

Viola consented reluctantly. She figured that since she had been receiving nothing but bad news all day, a little bit more wouldn't matter much. Albert returned to the phone and told Bob that it was all right for him to come right over.

Fifteen minutes later Bob Haines arrived at their door with a big grin on his face. In one hand he carried a bouquet of roses for Viola, and in the other hand a bottle of expensive champagne.

"I'm not the person the FBI is after. We came right over to celebrate the good news," he announced triumphantly in the doorway, then he let go a big whoopee. He handed Rev. Flowers the flowers and champagne, and gave Albert a big warm bear hug. Tears of joy were in his gray eyes. Wearing a big smile also, his wife Alice stepped into view from the darkness of the porch. She had brought some cake and ice cream.

Viola gave Albert a befuddled look and he returned the same kind of look. They both verged on smiling but needed more information before they could join in Bob and Alice's celebration.

"What happened, Bob?" Viola asked as she stepped forward and took charge.

"I just left my lawyer's office. He said my investigation's over. That I now have nothing to worry about. That the FBI told him this afternoon they're investigating somebody else. From what I could gather, it has something to do with money laundering," Bob Haines told them, then explained the difference in being the target of an FBI investigation and a subject of the investigation. "My lawyer says I'm no longer a subject of any investigation," he repeated himself happily.

Bob Haines made himself right at home, taking down some glasses, while Alice put the ice cream and cake away until they were needed.

Viola smiled. Seeing Albert and Bob Haines so happy made her happy. After so much bad news of late, she found some relief in Bob Haines' good news. Bob Haines' not going to prison was much more important than her losing her radio show, she told herself. In truth, now that her radio show was over and done with, she was rather relieved that she no longer had that responsibility. She hadn't realized before how time-consuming her show had been. Her mind turned to all the things she was now free to do.

With all the jubilation in the Flowers household that night, one wouldn't have guessed that Albert was trailing badly in the polls.

Chapter Twenty-seven

Rev. Flowers was happily surprised to learn on the internet that her round-trip airfare was much cheaper than she had prefigured. "Now I can afford to stay at a hotel," she said to herself as she punched in her Visa card number and completed her online transaction. She now wouldn't have to stay with friends while in St. Louis.

Her upcoming trip troubled her tremendously, so much so that she started losing sleep over it. She was worried not because she was one of the key preachers on the program. She never suffered from nervousness or stage fright when preaching. Since a tot she was fearless before the public, and throughout her career all she had to do was prepare her sermon and then walk out to the pulpit where God took over from there. Yes, God, for it seemed the moment she headed for the stage the spirit of God would take over her body and deliver the message. She was never afraid because she knew she was merely his vessel.

Therefore, having to preach in St. Louis wasn't what bothered her. What worried her was that Rev. Manny Scott would be there. This was a fear she suffered whenever she went to an out-of-town religious event without Albert and Manny was expected be there. Now for three whole days and nights she would have to avoid him somehow. She simply didn't trust herself to be alone with him for that many days and nights.

Her fear of something romantic rekindling between them really started the last time Manny preached in Los Angeles and she attended his sermon without Albert, who had to work and couldn't go with her. That night Manny as usual preached magnificently. It was a wonderful evening of preaching and song, and afterwards she and Manny had a great dinner, which was followed by delightful conversation about old times. Then because his flight wasn't until later the next morning, he invited her to have breakfast with him at his hotel, and she accepted his invitation.

She didn’t see anything wrong with that, for when on the road she often had breakfast with close friends in her hotel room when she had an early flight out that day. It saved time by not having to dress to go out and it helped with packing. Nonetheless, later at home that night, fear set in and Viola Flowers began having second thoughts about having breakfast with Manny.

“Thank Jesus for that flat tire,” she sighed, relieved that her breakfast the next morning with Manny had to be canceled due to the flat. Fate had mercifully intervened, she thought, for there was a part of her that was just a little too eager to have breakfast with Manny alone in his hotel room. She shuddered when she recalled how close she came that morning to going to bed with Rev. Scott, something she had vowed would never happen again. Manny always had the ability to sexually arouse her just by looking at her. So instead of having breakfast with him that morning, she made a nice breakfast for Albert and herself, and gave a silent blessing for coming to her senses in the nick of time.

Now there she was, dreading her trip to St. Louis. “Viola, quit being silly. You know how to handle Manny. So don't worry about him. It'll turn out all right,” she tried to convince herself as she got up from her computer.

Chapter Twenty-eight

Her sleek bluish-silver Boeing 757 roared eastwardly above dark ominous clouds. Rev. Flowers was on her way to the convention in St. Louis. It felt good to get away from Los Angeles for a few days. The long trip across country would give her a little undisturbed time to think about Bishop Neely's request that she head the planning committee for Rev. Brooks' big meeting. It was a decision she hated making. Head the committee? She wasn't even sure she wanted to be involved with any of it.

She faced the window of the plane, and came face to face with herself in the glass. What Rev. Campbell had said to her reverberated disturbingly in her mind: "We must be very careful these days, Rev. Flowers. We don't want gay black preachers doing to the black Protestant Church what the gay white priests are doing to the Catholic Church." It was a very stupid remark, she thought, but it did raise some disquieting questions. Was Reggie gay? Was Rev. Bowman lesbian? For that matter, was Bishop Neely gay?

"You're being silly, Viola!" she chided herself harshly, "Don't get caught up in Rev. Campbell's gay-baiting. You're a much bigger person than that. We black people have much more important things to do."

Since her meeting with Bishop Neely in his bedroom that day, she had done much reading on the subjects of HIV and AIDS and learned there were indeed serious problems in the black community. Nonetheless, she still felt very uncomfortable about becoming involved in Rev. Brooks' undertaking. She doubted if many members of her church would approve of her doing so. Like many black folks in L.A., most members of her church were in deep denial about the AIDS problem in their community. They were like ostriches with their heads buried in the sand.

"Please, dear Lord, tell me what to do," she prayed woefully as she felt a headache coming on. She took a deep breath, put her head back, and closed her eyes. The airliner was now cruising smoothly. "I don't have to make that decision right now," she told herself before returning to reading her book.

She had too much on her mind to concentrate on her book, so she put it down. Her mind moved to her grandfather. "Would I be doing wrong to help Reggie with his project, Grandpa?" she asked him. In her mind's eye, his hard disapproving face warned her to stick to just God and the Bible and leave the wicked secular world alone. "You might be going too far this time, Viola. Stay out of it and leave that problem to the will of God," his stern voice told her. It was like he believed the world was flat and she was about to step off the edge of the earth. It disturbed her greatly to think that if her grandfather was alive today, he would probably be supporting narrow-minded preachers like Rev. Campbell.

As previously said, Viola's late father was more broad-minded than her grandfather. Yet while her father changed many things for the better during his reign as bishop of the Church of God & Spirit, he also could go only so far. Take the Civil Rights Movement, for instance. In the 1950s and 60s many black religious leaders braved snarling police dogs and cattle prods in civil rights marches, sit-ins, and jail-ins across America. That was the time when the Reverend Walter Fauntroy led desegregation activities in Washington, D.C., and the Reverend C. K. Steele fought Jim Crow laws in Tallahassee, and the Reverend C.T. Vivian organized civil rights workers in Tennessee. Most important, that was the time when Reverend James Lawson taught Dr. Martin Luther King, Jr., then a young doctor of divinity graduate, Gandhi's principles of nonviolence as a strategy to bring about social change.

That selfsame Dr. King would go on to become the icon of the Civil Rights Movement, and Rosa Parks would refuse to sit in the back of the bus, starting the Montgomery Bus Boycott. In general, it was a time in history when a legion of other black ministers, too numerous to name, risked their lives fighting for the equal rights of their people, the black people in this country. But not Viola's father. He tried to heed Dr. King's call from his Birmingham jail cell that all men of the cloth, including white ministers, make moral witness to America's struggle for equal rights, but the parochial forces in his church were too powerful to overcome. The leadership of the Church of God & Spirit didn't want to become involved in the Civil Rights Movement, and forbade its constituent churches from doing so as well.

Therefore, to avoid destroying the national church, Rev. Flower's father, even though he was the bishop of the church, gave up on his efforts to get the church to join Dr. King. Hence the Church of God & Spirit sat on the sidelines and watched the great Civil Rights Movement as a mere spectator.

"The biggest regret of my life was that we here at the Church of God & Spirit didn't join Martin in the greatest battle of our lifetime. I just couldn't get my board to back me," her father lamented years later. Incidentally, Rev. Flowers' grandfather and father both had been bishops of their church.

Now Rev. Flowers faced the same moral challenge, save it was the AIDS problem, not Civil Rights. Over the years as pastor, she had tried to lead her church out of the darkness of doctrinaire scripture and into the light of modern times, but her church was like a huge boulder that wouldn't budge. Moving it was next to impossible. The best she could do was to keep trying to nudge her congregation in the right direction. Like her late father before her, sometimes she was able to make changes, sometimes she wasn't.

Whenever she made a proposal to her board of trustees that was too radical, Elder Lloyd, her most trusted lieutenant, would give her a certain look from across the table that told her she was going too far for the congregation. She always heeded his counsel and backed off. He was very good at gauging the temperature of things.

She recalled the time when, after learning about Rev. Brooks' amazing work with the AIDS children, she suggested to her board that the church conduct a special fund drive to raise money to fight AIDS. Brother Malone, a conservative member of the church, got up in the meeting and blasted the idea with both barrels. It was like she had suggested having a bake sale for prostitutes.

"Money for AIDS, Sister Flowers? Are you suggesting we raise money for *those people*?" he said with a ghastly look.

Rev. Flowers knew what Brother Malone meant by *those people*. Under the mistaken notion that AIDS was a gay disease, he was ineluctably referring to the homosexual community.

As she was about to answer Brother Malone, Elder Lloyd gave her that look that told her to back off. She glanced nervously around the meeting and divined that most of the board members didn't want to touch the AIDS issue either. So she dropped it. She simply lacked the strength of conviction to press it.

"Praying for AIDS victims is one thing, Sister Flowers, but raising money for them is a totally different matter," Elder Lloyd explained to her after the board meeting.

Yet Rev. Flowers enjoyed some success on other fronts in making the church more progressive. By pointing out how the Christian Right always opposed anything that helped ordinary working people, she successfully kept her church from following reactionary white leaders like Rev. Jerry Falwell and Pat Robertson as some black churches had done. Her members appreciated the many gains that labor unions had won for them, and touching Social Security was anathema to them. For Social Security was the only thing the black community could really count on from month to month.

Now the AIDS Struggle had become her Civil Rights Struggle. Like her father vis-à-vis the Civil Rights Movement decades earlier, she had to decide what role, if any, her church would play in that struggle.

"What should I do, dear Jesus?" she sighed as she pondered what to tell Rev. Bowman, whom she had promised an answer upon her return. "Is it the right thing to do?" she asked herself, "And even if it's the right thing to do, can I win over my board?"

She thought long and hard about those difficult questions. Then she thought of the younger members of her church, and felt better. Every year more and more young members were ascending to positions of leadership in the church; young, more progressive-thinking people, more in touch with the times. Young people who wanted to break with old beliefs and traditions. "But are there enough of them to support me now?" she would wonder aloud.

Chapter Twenty-nine

Rev. Flowers arrived in St. Louis from Los Angeles two days before the conference officially opened. The committee she co-chaired wanted to get a head start on its difficult assignment of preparing recommendations on how the various black gospel churches could work more closely together without losing any of their individual autonomy. In the spring of that year, when asked to serve as co-chair of that committee, she jumped at the chance.

"I've always said that it's high time we gospel churches should start abridging our differences and start working together. All faiths and denominations are talking about unification except us gospel folks," she told the hosting bishop when accepting the appointment.

Of course, as with most things involving the organizing of human affairs, politics quickly became involved. A sizable group of ministers wanted to work more closely with conservative white Christian leaders like Jerry Falwell and Pat Robertson on issues like right-to-life, prayer in public schools, and school vouchers, while another much larger group, mostly Democrats, took a different position on those issues. Plus the latter group was leery of getting too close to white conservative Christian groups which they saw as having a rightwing agenda.

Because of this split on issues, as a compromise, leaders of the conference selected co-chairpersons to head that very important committee, since it was essential that the committee work with both factions. Rev. Flowers, who appealed to both groups because of her right-to-life and anti-gay views, and her moderate position on most other social and political issues, was agreed to by both groups as a suitable co-chairperson. The other co-chair was also a person that both sides could trust.

Although the committee worked hard all spring and early summer coming up with findings and recommendations for the late summer gathering, it needed the two extra days to polish its report for presentation to the full conference; consequently Rev. Flowers and her fellow committee members arrived in St. Louis a couple of days early.

The Midwest Conference went well. Although she saw Manny Scott every day at the conference, they were never alone. He did ask her to go to dinner with him a few times, but each time she politely declined.

On the last night of the conference, Rev. Manny Scott preached, and was the best preacher at the conference. Even in middle age he was still very imposing up there before that vast audience, thrilling the crowd with that faultless elocution of his, that strut, those grand hand gestures, and that big winning smile.

Viola had to smile to herself. For despite that his sermon was brilliant, Manny had gotten his prophets wrong. He had quoted St. Elizabeth in the First Chapter of the Gospel of St Luke as saying: "Blessed art thou among women and blessed is the fruit of thy womb." He identified St. Elizabeth as St. James's mother, whereas in fact she was St. John the Baptist's mother. What made the mistake so egregious was that he then proceeded with a long learned discussion of St. James. He made other biblical mistakes in that sermon that were just as serious.

Manny hadn't changed, she thought. Manny was still Manny. Going back to their Bible college days, he had always been weak in his scripture. "It's the sizzle that sells the steak," he would say and laugh it off back then.

"Manny isn't dumb. He just isn't a scholar," Viola used to say when explaining to friends why Manny Scott was the most popular leader on campus while being a below-average student.

The other celebrants at the conference, however, didn't seem to mind Manny's scriptural blunders. They were too enthralled by how he cited the scripture, and less perturbed about whether the usage was apt or biblically correct.

This was particularly true of the women in the audience who were probably too enamored by Manny's fantastic charm to care if he occasionally got things a little wrong. It was almost humorous, Rev. Flowers thought. When Manny preached, women would spread their hand fans and begin fanning themselves vigorously as though someone had suddenly turned the heater up too high. He always had that effect on women.

Men in the audience were nearly as bad. They saw Rev. Emanuel Scott as a real man's man, and were in awe of him. Most of them knew he had once been a NFL football player. He was a hotshot running back in high school who received some national attention, but upon graduating from high school, at the insistence of his father, he went to a Bible college rather than a regular university or college with a football program. When he graduated from Bible college, he walked into the Chicago Bears football training camp undrafted and unscouted, tried out for the team, and was enthusiastically signed up by the Bears as a running back, only to suffer a bad knee injury before the season started that sent him permanently back into the ministry to serve only God. So, of course, the men found no fault with his preaching. Like at college, they treasured his friendship, and liked basking in the shade of his great popularity, especially when the ladies were around.

Rev. Flowers, however, cared about his scriptural errors. She knew Manny had a brilliant mind when he bothered to use it. She had tutored him on the Bible in college, and pressured him constantly to study his Bible more. Whereas she always carried her Bible with her wherever she went on campus, Manny couldn't find his Bible most of the time. She scolded him repeatedly about the C's and D's he got in his Bible courses, because she knew he could get A's and B's like she did, if he only applied himself more.

"Manny, you must study harder. Out in the real world, you can't get by on charm alone. Your congregation will be looking to you for the word of God. And the word of God is in the Bible," she used to fuss at him while dragging him by the arm to the college library to study evenings.

Again, it wasn't that Manny Scott was dumb or anything. It was simply that he wasn't a scholar. (Many years later he would discover that he was dyslexic.)

Chapter Thirty

On the day after the conference ended, Rev. Flowers went to breakfast with her St. Louis friends with whom she had spent scant time due to the rush of the conference. Later that afternoon she attended a back yard barbecue thrown for her by some other good friends in St. Louis. Her plans after the conference were to spend a couple of days in St. Louis with her friends there before flying home.

The weather was beautiful for the barbecue that afternoon. Amos Burke, the husband of her childhood friend Betty, was minding the grill. "Vi, I'm going to pack up a few bottles of my barbecue sauce so you can take them back to California with you for Al," the jolly-faced man said after Viola remarked about how good his spareribs smelled cooking on the fire. Amos took great pride in his barbecue, especially his sauce.

Albert Flowers loved Amos' sauce and once wanted to market it. Once when Amos and Betty were visiting the Flowers in Los Angeles, Albert and Amos spent that entire weekend talking about their forming a partnership and selling Amos' barbecue sauce to the nation's supermarkets. In their roughly sketched-out business plan Albert would be the CEO and chairman of the board, and Amos would be company president. (This was before Albert went into business with Bob Haines.)

But when Amos and Betty returned home to St. Louis, Amos became chickenhearted and started dragging his feet, which caused Albert to eventually give up on the deal.

"D'you see now what I mean, Vi. Black people are all talk and no action," Albert said cynically. Later, using Amos as an example, he made unfavorable comparisons to his new white Republican friends who seemed less afraid to take chances on good business opportunities. And Bob Haines later proved to be a prime example of that point.

Even after backing out of his deal with Albert, whenever anyone would listen to him, Amos Burke would still talk about someday selling his barbecue sauce in supermarkets across the nation. He blamed his wife Betty, not himself, for not going forward in his deal with Albert.

"Betty thinks the deal's too risky. It would take all the money we have. So I think I'll take a rain check," he told Albert on the phone that day when he backed out of the deal. Albert had been pestering him for months for certain market information he needed for their business plan.

It wasn't true that his wife Betty ruined the deal. Although she was apprehensive about the idea, she pretty much stayed out of it. Because of the high regard she had for Viola, Betty was rather honored that Amos was going into business with Albert, a person she respected highly. And she was glad Viola had married Albert, and not Manny Scott whom she disliked deeply. Her only worry was that Amos and Albert's partnership might adversely affect her friendship with Viola. "I've seen too many friends go into business together, only to end up hating each other afterwards," Betty told Amos fearfully.

Viola felt the same way. She never believed that people's going into business together, especially good friends, was as easy and simple as Albert and his Republican friends would have you believe. Fortunately, even though the barbecue sauce deal fell through, the two couples remained good friends. In that regard they were lucky.

"Thanks you for the sauce, Amos," Rev. Flowers said as she stood at the barbecue grill watching him cook. She was speaking of the bottles of sauce that Amos planned to send Albert. Her thanks for the sauce was lukewarm because she didn't really need anymore stuff in her luggage, especially stuff that might leak.

Viola and Amos talked and joked as she watched him turn the ribs over on the grill.

Then a late arrival opened the side gate and entered the back yard causing a stir among the people at the barbecue. Viola turned, and to her astonishment she saw Manny Scott headed her way.

"Oh no! What's he doing here?" she exclaimed to herself.

She thought she had gotten out of the woods safely when she shook his hand last night at the farewell reception and wished him a safe trip back to Chicago. Last night in the middle of the floor, he held her hand boldly and begged her shamelessly to have dinner with him later. His flight home wasn't until in the morning, he told her; he knew she was staying on in St. Louis for a day or two.

"Just for old time sake," he said in a small pleading voice, as he stood there in the center of the crowded hall gently stroking her hand, where people who saw them probably thought he was bestowing heavenly blessings on her, whereas in truth she knew he was trying to turn her on. Trying to weaken her resolve not to have dinner with him.

She retrieved her hand. "I would love to have dinner with you, Rev. Scott, but friends of mine who live here in St. Louis are picking me up in a few minutes, and they have other things planned for me," she said truthfully.

Before leaving Los Angeles a few days ago she resolved to keep her relationship with Manny Scott strictly on a formal basis. She would return to addressing him formally as "Rev. Scott," and would expect the same courtesy from him. She had learned a lesson from letting her guard down with him that night in Los Angeles when she nearly ended up in his hotel room for breakfast. Manny was very smooth and he knew what it took to get her sexually excited. He had that ability since their college days.

Now she stood there at the barbecue grill in disbelief, as she watched him glad hand his way across the yard towards her. Manny was his usual magnificent self as he won new admirers on his way over. When he saw Viola standing at the grill with Amos, he flashed that big beatific smile of his and pretended to be surprised to see her.

"Rev. Flowers, I thought you'd be halfway back to California by now," he said as he moved toward her, his expensive suit creased to a tee, his shoes glistening like polished glass.

"Manny, what are you doing here!" she cried out angrily, not trying to hide her displeasure.

Because she felt he had followed her, his pretense of being surprised irked her to no end. The way he lied about it. The big phony. He knew she wasn't returning immediately to Los Angeles after the conference. In their brief conversation at the farewell reception last night, she told him that she planned to stay a day or two in St. Louis, and while the convention hall was crowded and very noisy, she was sure he heard her.

She wondered who told him about the barbecue. She was certain it wasn't her friend Betty. When Betty picked her up at the auditorium last night after the farewell reception, Betty waved to Manny from her car without actually speaking to him. Manny must have put two and two together and guessed it was Betty Burke with whom she was spending the remainder of her time in St. Louis. Since he too had many good friends in St. Louis, it would have taken only a phone call or two to learn about the barbecue, another example of how small the world really was for black folks.

Manny Scott knew Betty from their college days when she visited Viola at the Bible college. From the start Betty and Manny disliked each other intensely.

Standing there in the back yard, Viola Flowers and Rev. Scott chatted inanely for awhile until Betty rescued her by calling her into the kitchen on the pretense of needing her help in there. Betty had sensed from Viola's lemon face that she was very unhappy about Manny's being there.

"Thank Betty. I just wasn't in the mood for any of Manny's nonsense right now," Viola thanked her old friend for saving her from her ex-lover.

She and Betty speculated that Betty's neighbor Rev. White was the one who told Manny about the barbecue. Manny then put two and two together and brazenly invited himself to the affair. He had that ability to make himself right at home with strangers.

In the kitchen Viola grabbed an apron and began helping wash the dishes from the back yard.

The back yard was now filled with latecomers to the barbecue. Amos Burke had put on another slab of ribs.

****

Early that evening everyone at the barbecue hurried indoors because of the mosquitoes. Viola Flowers was still in the kitchen with Betty helping out while discussing old times. It was nice being alone, just the two old friends. Manny poked his head into the kitchen several times and inquired if there was anything he could do to help, but each time he was politely chased back to the living room.

When finished cleaning up the kitchen, Viola untied her apron, washed her hands, applied some lotion to them, and then she and Betty sat down at the kitchen table where they continued talking about old times. Betty's guests, or what was left of them, were now in the parlor where Manny Scott was grandly holding court with everyone enraptured by his charm and wit.

Now it was nearly eight-thirty. Rev. Flowers reached for the telephone to call a cab, but Betty stopped her. "I'll have Amos drive you to your hotel," she said sadly, finally giving up on trying to persuade Viola to stay a few more days.

Betty walked to the doorway of the living room and called for Amos to take Viola to her hotel. The living room was now divided by gender, with the women gathered in one group, and the men hurdled laughing and thigh-slapping in another group. She had just assumed that Amos was in there with the men.

"Amos left a few minutes ago to take old Mrs. Haywood home," someone in the living room replied.

"Oh my," Betty sighed with disappointment because Mrs. Haywood lived on the far side of town.

Rev. Scott stepped from the male pack and volunteered magnanimously, "Viola can ride to the hotel with me. I was just about to call a cab. She and I can share it." His face brightened at this unexpected opportunity. Betty looked at Viola for guidance.

Viola shrugged her shoulders hopelessly and began gathering her things. Sharing a cab with Manny was probably her best choice. Their hotels were only a couple of blocks apart.

They rode a few blocks in the cab in total silence, with both of them being very uncomfortable. Manny was unusually quiet. Then he finally spoke up, "During the conference I was hoping we'd have a chance to talk, but I could never catch you alone."

"The last few days have been very hectic for both of us," Viola answered frostily.

"Have you been deliberately avoiding me? Like this afternoon at the barbecue, for instance, when you ran into the kitchen and hid all afternoon."

"I wasn't hiding. Betty and I had lots to catch up on."

"Have I done something to upset you?"

"No, of course not. Why would you say that?" she said defensively.

He was right. She had avoided him. Sitting there in the rear seat of the cab, with the lights and sounds from the various neighborhoods whizzing by, she painfully realized the cruel truth: today had nothing to do with anything Manny had done. He had done nothing. Manny had just been Manny. It was the distrust of herself that made her so fearful of him, causing her to behave like a silly teenager. That was the naked truth, and it was very painful. For she had always regarded herself as a very brave person.

She recalled what her father told her once about fear. "Fear increases when you run from it, and decreases when you face it squarely. So always face up to the things you fear, Viola. Throw a beam of light on them, and they'll probably vanish," he told her, and even as a child this advice made much sense to her.

"Quit berating yourself, Viola Flowers," Rev. Flowers scolded herself in the cab, "Your avoiding Manny today wasn't being cowardly. It was only being prudent." She took a deep breath and tried to relax.

When the taxicab stopped in front of her hotel to let her out, Manny said, "Why don't we stop at that coffee shop so we can talk." He pointed to the coffee shop in Viola's hotel that lit up the corner of the building like a bright globe. “My hotel's just down the street and I can walk from here.”

While handing the driver some money, Viola said, “Rev. Scott, I would love to, but I'm very tired. Besides, I've an early flight out in the morning and I have packing to do. And so do you.” A little voice inside her warned her not to weaken.

Before agreeing to share the cab, not wanting to feel obligated to Manny for the ride, she had insisted on paying her half of the fare, including the tip. Moreover, she had figured that he would want to stop somewhere along the way or come up to her room, supposedly to talk. She had prepared her declination in advance. On the taxi trip to the hotel she had remarked about how sleepy and tired she was. “I must be getting old. I used to be able to dance, sing and preach for days on end without giving it a second thought. Now after only a few days on the road, I'm dragging like a snail. I can't wait to get to the hotel so I can put this old body to bed,” she had told him early in the cab ride, hoping he would get the message.

Truthfully she was a little tired. In their younger days she and Manny could dance, clap, sing and shout in church for hours. Manny had a cute little Lindy Hop step that he had perfected which resembled Michael Jackson's "moon-walk" dance, except that Manny would dip his knees and pick up his clap on a certain beat in the song that gave him a few extra bounces. She had a cute little "standing in place" thing that she did when the hot gospel music moved her. Clapping and swaying, she would take on the happy look of someone being playfully tickled by God. Those were the good old days—the days when she believed that God had sent her Manny Scott as something very special.

The cabbie craned back over his shoulder to see what Rev. Scott was going to do. Poised to get out of the taxi also, Manny Scott pleaded, “Please have coffee with me, Vi. Just one cup, I promise. There is something very important I want to talk to you about.”

"Please, Rev. Scott, don't! Just don't!" she shrieked at him angrily, backing away with her hands out as if fending off an attacker.

Her shriek caused the cab driver's eyes to buck fearfully. She was nearly in tears.

Stunned by her bizarre reaction, Rev. Scott instructed the cabbie to take off, leaving her standing there alone on the sidewalk in front of her hotel.

In the elevator to her hotel room, she felt terrible about how she had just treated Manny. She wanted to cry. It was all a blur. "What happened out there a few minutes ago?" she asked herself foggily. It happened so quickly that she couldn't recall exactly what she had done or said to him out there on the sidewalk. All she knew was that for no reason at all she exploded. Manny had done nothing wrong. All he did was ask her to have a cup of coffee with him. He hadn't been knavish about it. She was the one who had acted childish, and she felt very ashamed of herself.

"Please forgive me, Manny," she said to herself pitifully as she fumbled for her room key.

Tired and confused, she entered her hotel room and had a good cry. Manny always had that effect on her.

She began filling the tub for a badly needed bubble bath, then the door bell rang. Thinking it was room service with the Alka-Seltzer she had ordered, she went to the door in her bathrobe and bare feet and opened it.

To her surprise, there stood Manny Scott looking frazzled like someone wanting in from the rain.

"What are you doing here!" she cried out in the doorway.

"I must talk to you, Vi." he said wretchedly, ignoring her hostile reception.

"If you don't leave, Rev. Scott, I'm going to call the manager!!" she warned him angrily.

"Viola, what in the world's wrong with you!" he asked her with wide eyes.

Like a slap in the face, Manny's brusqueness brought her to her senses. The haze lifted. Before her stood not the cocky, silver-tongued prince of the gospel, but a lost little boy. Manny appeared frightened and fragile. He looked like he would disintegrate into a thousand little pieces if she touched him. Standing there before her was someone clearly in need of help.

She stepped politely to one side. "Please excuse my ill-temper, Manny. Please come in and have a seat while I shut off my bath," she said and left the room. She went into the bathroom, closed the door behind her, and shut her bathwater off. Hyperventilating, she tried to catch her breath as she gazed into the steamed-up mirror and admonished herself to be brave.

"You can handle Manny, Viola. Go out there and hear him out. Go out there and get this over with," she lectured herself sternly before leaving the bathroom, recalling what her father had said about always facing your fears.

She took a seat across from him and gave him her full attention. Her headache was now gone. Her face was hard and serious. His face was soft and sad. She could see that his sadness was genuine, and she was deeply touched by that sadness.

"Madelene and I are getting a divorce," he sprung the surprise.

"A divorce?"

"Yes. We've been separated for months now."

"I'm sorry to hear that, Manny," Viola said with sincerity.

She had no idea that he and his wife were having marital problems. Her first thought was that it was fortunate that they didn't have children. Her first impulse was to sympathize with Madelene. Viola knew more than anyone else in the world how difficult loving Manny Scott was. All the many reasons that had caused her to break up with him, not once but many times, were probably now torpedoing his marriage to Madelene. Hence she couldn't help from feeling sorry for Madelene, the youngest wife of Manny's three marriages.

"I really made a mess of things this time, Vi. I don't want to lose Madelene. I love her too much," he moaned as his eyes filled with tears. "Please help me. What can I do to save my marriage?" he begged her.

She wanted to say: "*This time*, Manny? You made a mess of things *this time*? This would be your third divorce," but she didn't say it; she didn't have the heart to say it. She could see how badly he was bleeding, and she didn't want to hurt him more.

Knowing Manny like she did, she suspected what the main problem was, but she pulled her chair closer to him and let him talk. She was astonished by his frankness. His honesty in stepping up and taking full blame for his failing marriage. He told her about all of Madelene's grievances, as well as all his peccadilloes.

What Viola heard surprised her, yet it didn't surprise her. As someone once engaged to him, she recognized most of those faults instantly. They were mostly the same failings that she and Manny used to argue about all the time. The same faults that had made her cry more times than she cared to remember. It was strange sitting there hearing that her worst fears about Manny had come true for another woman.

"That's not the worst of it, Vi. Madelene's five months pregnant," he added hopelessly.

"Oh Sweet Jesus!" Viola let out a little catlike cry.

The two of them then talked for hours. Her dear friend of yesteryear had returned, and it was like old times back in Bible college. When she spoke he listened with the intensity of someone taking notes. She hadn't realized that he loved Madelene so. During their talk he gallantly fought back the tears, and teary-eyed herself, she hugged him. She was very proud of him for accepting his responsibility like a man. Maybe he had finally grown up.

"Now that you know what you must do, Manny, you must ask the Lord for the strength to do it. I'll pray with you," she told him, and both of them, tired and drained of emotions, dropped to their knees and prayed. Both weeping.

She thanked the Lord for giving her Albert.

****

After Manny left, she lay in bed till the wee hours of the morning unable to sleep because of what he had told her. She realized what a fool she had been in recent months. Since her close call with him in Los Angeles that morning, she had been afraid of Manny. How stupid of her. It hadn't been a close call at all. She was the problem, not him. There would have been nothing wrong with her having breakfast with Manny in his hotel room that morning, and nothing would have happened. She realized that now.

Questions now began to swirl in her head. Did she intend, unconsciously or otherwise, to go to his hotel room that morning in L.A. to seduce him? To have sex with him? Was that why she had gotten all dressed up, lipstick and the rest, that morning? Was it lust? She remembered a sermon she gave once on lust, one of the seven deadly sins.

It was lust, she concluded. Lust and pride and the still-warm embers of an old love. Since that day in Los Angeles, her relationship with Manny had alternated between fear and anger. Mostly fear—fear that she would be too weak to resist temptation. To resist lust. To resist him. And she had unfairly blamed him. She was angry at him because of the guilt she felt for lusting in her heart for him. All along she had been the culprit, not Manny. Now she realized what a dear friend he was, a fact she had forgotten of late.

She finally dropped off to sleep, but not before telling Manny, as though he was actually there, that she was very sorry, and she asked his forgiveness. She also thanked Jesus for bringing her to her senses.

Chapter Thirty-one

When Rev. Flowers arrived home from her trip, Albert had already left for work. She could see from the wetness of the grass that he had watered the lawn before leaving. Inside the house she put her luggage down and smiled. The kitchen was spic and span. All the waste baskets had been emptied, and all her plants had been recently watered. She kicked off her shoes and went back to her study where many messages were waiting for her on her answering machine, including calls from Rev. Evelyn Bowman, Bishop Neely, and someone from KWCP. In fact, Evelyn Bowman had called three times.

In her last voice-mail messages Rev. Bowman said: "I'm sorry to be pestering you like this, Rev. Flowers. You said you would give us your answer when you got back. I'm just checking to see if you returned yet. Please call me as soon as you can."

In his message Bishop Neely wanted to know if she had talked to Rev. Bowman yet. He mentioned again how much he was looking forward to working with her. He left not only his office number, but his home number as well. The man from KWCP wanted her to call him back, saying it was very important. It was clear to Rev. Flowers that everyone was anxiously waiting for her. Her time was running out. She had to make a decision.

"Oh mercy!" she moaned to herself as she marched upstairs to unpack.

The telephone rang.

"Is this Rev. Flowers? Hello, Rev. Flowers. We've never met. I'm Bernie Graham, the new program director at KWCP. I replaced Larry Logan," the deep male voice on the other end of the phone said.

"Yes," she answered icily. She was still angry at KWCP for what they did to her and the other programmers at the station. Then it dawned on her what he had just said. The last time she talked to

Larry Logan, he feared he would be fired too, and at the time she said a little prayer for him. It turned out that he was right.

"We want you back, Rev. Flowers," the man said, "We were too hasty in canceling your show. Please come back. I'm sure we can work out satisfactory terms."

"May I get back to you on that, Mr. Graham? I just returned from a trip out of town, and I'm still trying to catch my breath," she told him. Truthfully she didn't want to deal with that problem right now. It simply lacked priority and seemed unimportant relative to her other problems, other problems like Rev. Reggie Brooks' people waiting anxiously by their phones for her to call them. KWCP was the least of her worries.

"Yes, of course. I understand. Call me as soon as you can," the new program director said before hanging up, disappointed.

"Oh, sweet Jesus! What's happening to my life?" Viola uttered to herself, feeling the events of recent days crushing her.

Her father looked up from his photo on her desk and told her to slow down, collect herself, and take one thing at a time. "Take first things first, Viola," his sympathetic eyes seemed to say, "Call Rev. Bowman and Bishop Neely, and give them an answer. It's irresponsible to keep them waiting."

She could see her father was thinking about the time when he was in a comparable situation regarding the Civil Rights Movement years ago. The Rev. Dr. Martin Luther King, Jr. called him one day and asked him to join them in the Movement, and he told Dr. King that he would get back to him with an answer. As he promised, he got back to Dr. King with his answer, which was "no," an answer he would rue for the rest of his life. His church had voted not to become involved in the Civil Rights Movement. "It's not our problem. It's God's problem," they in effect said.

For the rest of his life he regretted that he and the national Church of God & Spirit stood on the sidelines while Dr. King and other black preachers fought for Civil Rights. All his life he felt he didn't do enough to persuade his church to get involved.

Rev. Flowers knew her father felt he had flunked the most important test in his life by not joining Rev. Martin Luther King,

Jr. Would she flunk the biggest test of her life? Was the AIDS' fight her Civil Rights challenge?

She recalled the advice her father gave her once about good leadership. "Be a strong forceful leader, yes, but don't let your zeal take you in directions that your followers are unprepared to go. Many an emperor has been toppled from power for ignoring this simple truth," he said. She recalled something else he said in conjunction with that. "It's the job of a good leader to prepare his followers for what's ahead. These two propositions might seem contradictory, but they aren't. The former instructs the leader what he or she must do with respect to the latter," her father added.

If she joined Rev. Brooks and Bishop Neely, would she be taking her followers where they were unprepared to go? She realized that not just her church, but the entire black religious community was terribly divided on the issue of AIDS and homosexuality. She recalled reading somewhere that the head bishop of the African Methodist Episcopal Church, after the white Episcopal Church confirmed its first openly gay bishop, ordered that a statement be read in all AME churches that the AME Church did not support the ordination of openly gay persons.

She thought of Rev. Owens' remark awhile back about Rev. Brooks. "Rev. Flowers, I just don't know about Brother Brooks. Some folks are saying that he's a 'down-low' boy himself," Rev. Owens said. At Rev. Brooks' big meeting Rev. Owens was among the preachers who stormed out angrily before the meeting barely got underway. She recalled what Reggie Brooks told her once. "Vi, you're the reason I became a preacher. You showed me how much good a person of God can do in the community." That day he had just become an ordained minister.

She saw now that the issue had nothing to do with whether or not Reggie Brooks was homosexual. Reggie was no part of any conspiracy. The truth was that he became a person of the cloth because of her. She was the one who had inspired him to do good in the community. Poor Reggie. Now he was being viciously attacked for merely doing the Lord's work. Would anyone doubt that if alive today Jesus would be at Rev. Brooks' side in his fight against AIDS.

Rev. Flowers reached for the telephone and dialed. "Hello, Rev. Bowman. I got your messages. My trip went well, thank you. Yes, praise the Lord. Yes. I've made my decision. I would be delighted to work with Bishop Neely. When do you want to meet? Fine. I'll see you then."

After she hung up she looked at her grandfather on the wall. His countenance seemed puzzled. She looked at her father's photo on her desk and his smile seemed to have gotten wider.

Chapter Thirty-two

Rev. Flowers and Bishop Neely arrived at Rev. Brooks' planning meeting at the same time. He held the door open for her. "Beauty before age," the octogenarian chuckled as he stepped aside and allowed her to enter the room first.

"Thank you, Bishop Neely," she said gaily.

The meeting hadn't started yet. Rev. Brooks met them at the door and thanked them for coming. Waiting for things to get underway, Rev. Evelyn Bowman and some other ministers were standing around chatting. The purpose of the meeting was to prepare an agenda with recommendations for the big meeting of all the black preachers in Los Angeles next month. It was Bishop Neely's idea that they, the organizers, should hit the ground running at the big meeting. It was their second chance, and they couldn't afford to blow it.

"The quicker we can give people work to do, the better our chances of avoiding rancor and dissension," Bishop Neely had said to Rev. Brooks when broaching the idea. Then he kidded, "Please believe me, we black preachers can be really quarrelsome if not kept busy."

Rev. Flowers took a seat next to Bishop Neely. She didn't know most of the other ministers at the table. Before the meeting began, one man remarked offhandedly to her, "I hear your radio show's been cancelled. It's a pity. I really liked your show. If still on the air, that show could really help us now." Others within earshot concurred.

Rev. Flowers broke into a big smile. "I'm not being cancelled. My program returns on the tenth. I survived reorganization at the station. I think someone higher up took another look at my ratings and realized their mistake."

Her smile got wider. "What's great is, I'm returning to the station on my terms. And one of the things I asked for and got was an additional hour each week devoted only to the AIDS problem.

Management loved the idea. They promised me the necessary resources so we can send a reporter out into the community with a tape recorder to do personal stories on people affected by AIDS. The afflicted. The love ones. The children. The caretakers. The hospitals. These reports will be aired each week on my extended show, and at the end of each segment, we'll try to offer some helpful solutions."

At the head of the table Rev. Brooks leaned forward and listened with rapt attention, as did Bishop Neely and the others.

"You'll still have gospel music, I hope?" a minister asked her from across the table. Her music was the main reason he listened to her show. Rev. Flowers played tapes, records and CDs of gospel artists that couldn't be heard on the air anywhere else.

"Oh my yes. Good music and prayer will remain the staples of my show," she laughed.

Before Rev. Brooks called the meeting to order, Bishop Neely leaned over, cupped his mouth and said to Viola Flowers softly, "Rev. Brooks has asked me to serve as chair of the big meeting. Because of my recent illness, I'm going to need help. Would you serve as co-chair?"

"I'd be honored," she answered without hesitating.

"We won't be left on the sidelines this time, Daddy," Rev. Viola Flowers smiled to herself as the meeting came to order.

Afterward

Rev. Flowers will be returning soon in *The Bishop's Granddaughters*, another novel in my trilogy of novels that examine strong, interesting women at home, at work, at worship, and at play, including their love lives. As you know from this novel, Rev. Viola Flowers is a highly respected pastor (I guess we can say that now) of a church in Los Angeles. One summer she returns home from a family reunion in the Deep South with an old dog-eared Bible that relatives at the reunion claimed was her late grandfather's Bible, and upon examining it closely she discovers that certain pages had been ripped out. "What happened years ago so horrendous that our family history had to be torn from the family Bible?" she wonders with alarm. She's so troubled by the obliterated material that she travels to the South to investigate her family history. And she's not prepared for what she finds there—a grisly double murder in 1910. "Sweet Jesus, was grandpa involved in those awful murders?" she moans to herself. Her grandfather was a legendary bishop in the Church of God & Spirit. Her father was also a prominent minister in that church. This is not a thriller or murder mystery. It's a novel about a courageous lady preacher whose religious faith must carry her through many serious challenges, including the possible disgrace of her family.

The Bishop's Granddaughters will be available soon at Amazon and other bookstores where good books are sold. Pre-order now and be the first in your circle to see what Rev. Flowers is up to next.

****

Author WILL GIBSON founded the American Black Book Writers Association as its first president and trade journal editor-in-chief. He served on the advisory board of "Black Authors: Selection of Sketches from Contemporary Authors, Gale Research. He is the author of many novels, including *Lola & The World Of Buddy Shortt.*

Book cover was designed by Ezekiel Sweetz, and the "A Woman's Silhouette" cover image was legally acquired from YOY Images.

Made in the USA
Charleston, SC
14 January 2013